SUNDAY

by Georges Simenon

Translated by Nigel Ryan

Harbrace Paperbound Library

A Helen and Kurt Wolff Book | Harcourt Brace Jovanovich

New York and London

Library of Congress Cataloging in Publication Data

Simenon, Georges, date
Sunday.

(Harbrace paperbound library ; HPL 68)
Translation of Dimanche.
"A Helen and Kurt Wolff book."
I. Title.
PZ3. S5892Sx7   [PQ2637.I53]   843'.9'12   75-29341
ISBN 0-15-686301-4

First Harbrace Paperbound Library edition 1976

A   B   C   D   E   F   G   H   I   J

SUNDAY

ONE

He had never needed an alarm, and he had been conscious for some time already, with his eyes shut, of the sun filtering in between the two narrow slits in the shutters, when he finally heard a muffled ringing in the room above.

It was a narrow attic, directly above his head. He knew every corner of it, the iron bedstead and its dark red coverlet, the washbasin on a carved three-legged wooden stand and the enamel jug on the floor, the scrap of brown matting which was never in place, and he could have sketched the outline of the stains on the whitewashed walls, the narrow black picture frame surrounding a Virgin Mary in a sky-blue dress and hanging crooked.

He knew, too, the half-wild, spicy smell of Ada, who was always slow to rouse herself from sleep. She had not yet stirred. The alarm was still ringing and Émile was becoming impatient. His wife, motionless beside him in the big walnut bed, must have heard it too, but she would say nothing, would not move so much as her little finger: that was all part of her tactics.

From now onwards it did not matter. The day had come; he had known it without opening his eyes, even before noticing that the sun had risen, or hearing the piping of the birds and the cooing of the two white pigeons.

Ada, upstairs, was turning over in one movement, stretching out a brown arm, her nightdress open to the middle of her bosom, groping with her hand on the marble top of the bedside table.

Sometimes she was so heavily asleep that she would knock over the alarm clock, and it would go on ringing on the floor, but this did not happen today. The ringing stopped. There was another moment of silence, of stillness. At last her naked feet, on the floor, hunted for her slippers.

If Émile had been asked what he was feeling that morning he would have had difficulty in answering. He had been pondering about it before the alarm went off. To tell the truth he did not feel any different from other days, other Sundays. He was not afraid. Nor had he any desire to retreat. He was not impatient, nor excited. He could hear, behind him, the regular breathing of his wife, was aware of her warmth, her smell as well, which he had never grown used to, so different from Ada's, a smell which, toward morning, impregnated the bedroom, at once stale and acrid like sour milk.

In the attic, Ada did not wash. It was not until later, when the bulk of her work was done, that she would go upstairs again for her toilet. She did not put on stockings, or panties, contented herself with pulling on a reddish cotton dress over her nightdress, which was short.

She could barely have passed a comb through her thick black hair before she opened the door and started down the stairs, sometimes going back a step to retrieve a slipper.

She brushed against his door as she passed, reached the ground floor, and he could still hear her; although even if he had not heard he would have been able to follow her movements in his thoughts, so well did he know the household routine.

She was going into the kitchen, with its red tiling, turning the big key in the glass door before opening the shutters and revealing the clear blue sky, the two gnarled olive trees, the pines beyond the terrace, and, in a hollow between the hills, the gleaming roadstead which led into the harbor of La Napoule.

The two pigeons would be scratching about for food, like hens, in the gravel. Ada stood still for a moment, gradually waking up, gathering strength from the freshness of the morning, and Madame Lavaud must by now have left her little house at Saint-Symphorien, near Pégomas, and begun the climb up the path.

Émile had plenty of time. Bells were ringing, at Pégomas or

Mouans-Sartoux. A car was passing somewhere nearby. Ada was lighting the butane heater and grinding the coffee.

It was the day, the Sunday he had fixed a long time ago, but there was nothing to stop him from going back on his decision, letting things go on as they had been going on for almost a year now.

No such temptation came into his head. The idea never occurred to him that he was free to put everything back once again into the melting pot.

His pulse was beating normally. He was not afraid. He was not overawed. When he finally got up, at the moment when Ada, downstairs, was pouring the water into the coffee and Madame Lavaud's footsteps could be heard, he glanced at his wife, of whom he could see only the shape of her body beneath the sheet, her hair dyed blonde, a pink ear, a closed eye.

It was she who had insisted that there should be no outward changes, that they should go on sleeping in the same room, in the same bed, which had been her parents' bed, so that it did happen, on some nights, that their bodies involuntarily came into contact.

On tiptoe, from habit rather than from fear of waking her, he went into the bathroom and shaved, just as he always did in the morning on Sundays and market days. On other days he came back upstairs later on, like Ada, to wash and shave.

Downstairs the two women were talking in low tones, sitting at the table, having their breakfast.

It was the end of May. There had been heavy rains in April, then some weeks of cold, with the *mistral* blowing three days out of four. A week ago summer had started; the *bise* in the morning blew from the east, to veer slowly over the sea and, falling in the evening, it would leave the night in absolute stillness.

He did not know if Ada was looking at him in any other way than usual, since he avoided watching her. She served him his bowl of coffee, pushed the plate of pizza toward him, and he cut himself a large slice which he ate standing up, looking out of doors, from the threshold.

She knew. He had not given her any details. They had never exchanged many words.

One day during the week, Tuesday, if he remembered rightly, he had simply said to her:

"Next Sunday."

She did not know why he had chosen a Sunday, nor why he had waited so long, almost a year. Had she thought he was afraid, or that he was sorry for Berthe?

"Are the baskets in the car?"

Apart from a vague good morning, Madame Lavaud had not opened her mouth and anyone might have thought she was a stranger in the house. She was a round, yet tough, little woman of sixty-two and she had three or four married children somewhere in France. Refusing to be a burden to them, she had for a long time been a maid in the service of a doctor in Cannes, then at a dentist's.

Two years earlier, she had married a second time a man Émile had never seen, whom nobody at La Bastide knew. She had met him, as far as could be gathered, walking in Cannes during one of her weekly days off, while he, a pensioner in the Old People's Home, was also having his Thursday walk.

He was seventy-two. For months she had been going to see him, taking him sweets. One morning everybody had been surprised to see Julia's name in the newspapers among the marriage banns.

Afterwards her husband went on living at the Home. She went on working at La Bastide.

Why had they married? She had never referred to it. Perhaps he had a little money she hoped to inherit? Perhaps she had acted out of pity?

Émile did not bother about it, as he was not one of those people who enjoy pondering and striving to create problems for themselves.

He had done nothing to bring about the present situation. It was not he who had set the drama in motion, and in the last resort he would have been hard put to it to say exactly how it had begun.

The difficulty, when one tries to remember things, is to distinguish between what counts and what does not. One is confronted by a litter of minute facts, some of which seem to be important, others to be insignificant; and then one sees one has got it all wrong, one tries to find other causes, realizing that those already discovered explain nothing.

Or else, if one is satisfied with oversimple explanations, one ends by reasoning like the newspapers which state:

"Because he was drunk, a lock-keeper has hacked his wife to death with a knife."

Why was he drunk? And why a knife? Why his wife? Above all, why does nobody ask whether she was not a natural victim?

For if one admits the criminal type of a murderer, one may suppose there is also the type of the natural victim, all of which leads to the conclusion that, in crime, the man or woman killed deserved to be called to account quite as much as the man or woman who did the killing.

It is a complicated business, and Émile did not like thinking about complicated matters. Besides, as he ate his pizza and gazed at a stretch of the Mediterranean at the foot of the Estérel, he was not thinking seriously, or at least not in any *dramatic* fashion.

There were just odd scraps of ideas which floated into his mind. There was no question of solving a problem. He did not pretend to be able to explain things.

He had found himself in a predetermined situation, from which he had to emerge in one way or another. One single solution had occurred to him, one which seemed obvious.

All his efforts had been concentrated on perfecting this solution, which had taken time, just eleven months in fact.

Now that the day had come, it would do no good to re-examine the whole position. Besides, he had not the slightest temptation to do so. What, at most, gave him a strange sensation was to reflect, as the life of the household began in the same pattern as on other Sundays:

"This evening, it will all be over."

He was in a hurry to grow a few hours older. When he had finished his breakfast, still standing up, and lit his first cigarette, his hand was trembling slightly. Only then did his eyes meet those of Ada, who was pouring him out a second bowl of coffee, and he thought he read a question in them which irritated him.

He had told her:

"Next Sunday."

Now it was Sunday. She had nothing to feel uneasy about. She would have been wrong, moreover, to have a guilty conscience, for though she was involved in what was about to take place, she was not the principal reason for it.

She was, in fact, the accident. It could have begun in another way, with anybody else, or with nobody.

"I've made a little list for you, Monsieur Émile. Don't forget the Parmesan cheese. . . ."

Madame Lavaud, who had donned her coarse blue cloth apron, was filling a jug of water to go and wash the tiled floor of the dining room and the bar.

La Bastide was almost like a stage setting, a Provençal inn exactly as people from Paris and the North imagine an inn in the South, with a red paved floor, bricks showing around the windows, ocher walls and big glazed china vases. The bar was constructed on some old wine presses, and the tables in the dining room were covered, as a matter of course, with checked tablecloths.

The two residents, Mademoiselle Baes and Madame Delcour, who had just got up, would soon be down in their flowered or spotted dresses, large straw hats on their heads, to have their breakfast on the terrace.

They were both Belgian, in their sixties, and both came each year to spend two months on the Riviera.

Émile climbed into the driver's seat of his two-horsepower converted truck, and started the engine. When he turned around, just before the hill, he caught sight of Ada standing on the doorstep and felt no emotion.

The road was a difficult one, with a rock face to the right and a ditch to the left. He no longer noticed it. A little later he was driving along between two hedges, passing in front of a villa, then a small farm, to come out finally at Les Baraques, on the Route Napoléon.

Several motorcycles were climbing toward Grasse, and on most of them there were young couples. Some of their riders had already stripped off their shirts. Other cars passed him on the way down, with Paris, Swiss, or Belgian number plates.

At Rocheville he turned right, skirted the cemetery wall, then the hospital, went down the Rue Louis-Blanc and crossed the railway bridge. He took the same road three times a week, always tried first to park outside the butcher's, then, if he could not find a space in the narrow Rue Tony-Allard, near the light blue-fronted dairy where he took in his provisions.

The Forville market was in full swing, and to prove that the season had begun several women were to be seen in shorts, even bathing suits, dark glasses hiding their eyes, hats more or less Chinese in shape shading their heads.

It was good to be busy and to have these familiar sights passing before his eyes. He must not forget his list either.

"Well, Monsieur Émile? Many guests?"

The smells of cheeses. Fair-skinned sales-girls, with spotless white aprons.

"Two boarders, the same old ones."

"They won't be long now. Yesterday we had our first traffic jams on the road."

He felt in his pocket for the list, gave his order, deciphering with some difficulty Madame Lavaud's handwriting.

At heart he disliked her. She was a foreign element at La Bastide, and he was aware that he knew nothing about her, that she took no part in the life of the household, that she did her job, and nothing more, to make money.

The others too, perhaps. But not in the same way. For example, if Maubi, the gardener, cheated him, he would know how, why, and it would not even be a secret between them. He could have said to him outright:

"Maubi, you're a thief!"

Maubi would probably have smiled, winking as he did so.

The air was becoming hot. Émile moved from the shade into the sun, from the uproar of the market to the silence of the side streets. Opposite the dairy could be seen a shop selling fishing tackle. It was a month since he had been fishing. He would go as soon as it was all over. That reminded him that he had to make sure that Dr. Guérini's boat had left the harbor.

For he had foreseen everything. It was not for nothing that he had spent eleven months preparing for what was going to happen today.

All that time had been spent not in hesitations, but in reflections and minute calculations.

As he looked back, it seemed short. He was surprised, all of a sudden, to have arrived so near to the end, and, though he still had no temptation to shrink back, he was nonetheless seized with a certain giddiness.

With a basket in one hand he headed toward the harbor, not the yacht basin, where several white sails could be seen being unfurled, but the one with the fishing boats, where the *pointus*, which had gone out at night, were coming in to tie up alongside one another.

As he advanced among the nets stretched out to dry, he could hear:

"Morning, Émile. . . ."

For he was no longer a complete stranger.

He asked:

"Is Polyte back?"

"Half an hour ago. I think he's got something for you. . . ."

He crossed on to another landing stage and found Polyte, in his boat, busy sorting out fish.

"Have you got the calamaries?"

"Six pounds."

They formed a viscous mass of porcelain whiteness in the bottom of the basket, and some of the calamaries had disgorged their ink.

"Do you want some *bouillabaisse* as well?"

"At how much?"

"Don't get excited. We'll fix a price."

He took a certain amount because, with the fine weather, there was a good chance of there being about thirty lunches, and most tourists asked for *bouillabaisse*.

Dr. Guérini's boat was not at its mooring.

"Has the *Sainte-Thérèse* been gone long?"

"I saw her among the islands on my way in. He must have sailed in the dark."

The cheese, the fish, the meat. There remained the grocer's to call at. Then he pushed open the door at Justin's, one of the small bars in the market.

"Morning, Émile. . . ."

The men were drinking white wine, the women coffee, and it seemed that everybody was talking at once. They were market people, or shopkeepers from the square, who had been on their feet since three or four in the morning. The men all took their turn to go off toward the urinal.

"Nice day today!"

"Nice day!"

He was just a man like other men, a man like them. Nobody suspected. There was only Ada who knew, and Ada probably had a false notion of his motives.

Long before she began working at La Bastide, it was rumored in the neighborhood that she was not like other girls. If nobody actually claimed she was mad, she was considered at best as retarded.

Was this due to the fact that she seldom spoke and seemed to be afraid of people?

At any rate, she was not completely normal. She did not behave like girls of her age, and she did not mix with them any more than she mixed with boys.

"She's a savage?"

Her parents, too, lived like savages, cut off from the rest of the neighborhood.

When her father, Pascali, had set up house on the outskirts of Mouans-Sartoux, he already had gray hair, a face lined and baked by the sun, and he spoke only a half-intelligible mixture of Italian and French.

As he was a good mason, he found work all over the place, mostly repair jobs, for he worked alone.

He would disappear periodically for weeks at a stretch, then return and start work again.

On one of these reappearances he was accompanied by a woman of about forty, who looked like a gypsy, and a small girl of twelve who did not answer when she was spoken to.

Émile was barely twenty-five at the time and had just arrived at the Harnauds', who owned La Bastide and were to become his parents-in-law.

He could remember a skinny girl who in this sunny country was one of the few to be always dressed in black, a strange garb, moreover, half dress, half apron, which hung shapelessly upon her body.

People would come across her at a turning in a path, or in a wood, or beside the main road. They would say:

"It's the daughter of Pascali and that gypsy woman."

But there was nothing to prove that the woman Pascali had brought back with him was a gypsy. In actual fact, nothing was known, and Pascali offered no explanation. Were the local police any the wiser? Probably not, for they would have talked of it sooner or later.

Francesca did not mix with the other women, seldom left the house, which Pascali had eventually built between two jobs for his clients, and which looked unlike any other house.

It was as if he had tried to put together examples of every kind of construction he knew, examples too of all types of stone and other building materials.

People said he did not allow his wife to go out, that sometimes he shut her in and on various occasions beat her.

Francesca's face was deformed by two scars across her cheeks, and these were attributed to the Italian's jealousy. Some claimed he had deliberately disfigured his wife, to discourage would-be lovers.

Yet it was he who had taken his daughter, Ada, to La Bastide one day. Émile had already been married for some time. His father-in-law was dead. His mother-in-law had gone back to Vendée where her family was.

In his own dialect, which the Italians themselves could not understand, Pascali had discussed Ada's wages, her conditions of work, and it had all taken place in such a way that one might have thought he had come to sell her.

He had not asked, on her behalf, for any days off, or annual holidays. She never took any. She seldom went, even for a visit, to her parents' house, which was little more than a mile away, and

Pascali was content to appear after long intervals, covered in lime, and sit in the kitchen drinking a glass of wine and gazing at his daughter.

Was this how it had started, or must it be still further back?

On the beach, in front of the Carlton, the Majestic, the Miramar, people were already bathing, women were settling under sunshades, some of them surrounded by children, and rubbing oil into their bodies before exposing themselves to the sun.

In the covered market Émile met colleagues who kept restaurants in town or in the vicinity. Cars were streaming in from the Estérel and others, from the direction of Nice, were arriving from Italy.

It was all part of the preparations for a fine Sunday, which were taking place like the preparing of a restaurant, when the places are being laid and vases of flowers set in the middle of the tables. The flower market was in full swing as well. Émile needed to buy some. The truck was filling up gradually and the hands of the clock were moving slowly forward, bringing nearer the hour when he would have to act.

There had been no single beginning, but several. And one of these, no doubt, was what had happened one afternoon in the attic.

Ada had been working at La Bastide for nearly two years and must, therefore, have been eighteen. He was not yet thirty. He had never taken any interest in her, except, every now and then, to look at her with a frown and wonder what she was thinking.

You could give her any job to do without her complaining. She didn't work fast and she was not thorough, but nobody had any control over her, for when one made a remark to her, or when Berthe got angry with her, she remained as blank as a wall.

He remembered various scenes, with Berthe, exasperated, finally screaming at her, half hysterically:

"Look at me when I am speaking to you!"

Ada would gaze at her with dark, empty eyes.

"Do you hear me?"

She would not flinch.

"Say, 'Yes, madam.' "

She would repeat, indifferently:

"Yes, madam."

"Couldn't you be a little more polite?"

Émile almost believed that if his wife lost her temper so easily, it was because she could not succeed in reducing Ada to tears.

"Supposing I threw you out of the house?"

Still the stone wall.

"I shall speak to your father about it. . . ."

As for Émile, he had become accustomed to her, but rather in the way he would have become accustomed to the presence of a dog in the house. A dog does not speak either, does not always do what one would like to see it do.

Then, one afternoon when Berthe was away, he had gone up to the attic, without ulterior motives, because he was looking for Ada and she did not answer, and when he had come down again he did not know whether to be pleased or frightened by what had just taken place.

At any rate, he knew no more about her than before, and understood her perhaps less than ever.

He remembered above all a look which he had never seen in a woman before, rather similar to the look of an animal at the approach of a man.

That was three years ago now. Could he claim to know her better, and was this called love?

If a beginning is strictly necessary, then this was one among many others.

But as far as Berthe was concerned, the beginning was not to be found till two years later, at siesta time, on June 15th; he recalled the date, the hour, the smallest details.

Was it still important? Was it not all past and done with? He had had the time, in eleven months, to think about it, and yet he had been scarcely ever worried about it.

Even today, it did not disturb him unreasonably. He was not excited. He regretted nothing. He was not scared either.

A certain impatience, yes, which made him drink his coffee too hot at Justin's bar. A trembling of the fingers, as had happened this morning in the kitchen, and a floating sensation in the chest. But that could occur just as well when he was out fishing for *boulantin* and had a good catch at the end of his line.

And the sensation of unreality was familiar to him. When you are at sea, early in the morning, aboard a *pointu*, alone on the water which shines and breathes with a monotonous rhythm, you are no longer completely yourself, and it may happen that all this blue and this inhuman peace inspire you with a kind of anguish.

The Forville market was the same as on other Sundays, with its familiar faces, its noises, its smells. And yet was it not rather as if he had surveyed the scene through a mirror?

For several hours now he had not formed part with the rest of the world. This evening, tomorrow, he would once again be a man like the others. Not quite like them.

He must not think. One should never go over again what has been decided once and for all.

He had told Ada, without giving her any details:

"Next Sunday . . ."

It was now that Sunday. Everything was waiting. It was too late to stop events.

"I'll have a pack of Gauloises."

He lit one, slowly expelled the smoke. All he had to do was to collect the package from the butcher's where he had left his order as he passed.

At this hour Berthe would be busy with her toilet, in the bedroom, where she would have opened the shutters. The two boarders, Mademoiselle Baes and Madame Delcour, both of them blonde and fat, with thick, red arms, would be strolling one behind the other along a pathway, picking wild flowers, of which in due course they would come and ask him the names.

Occasionally they could be heard giggling like little girls. Mademoiselle Baes had inherited a biscuit business and her friend was the widow of a pork butcher.

On the Riviera it was as if they had returned to their childhood, and when the weather did not permit them to take walks they would spend hours writing postcards.

He tossed the butcher's package into the truck, closed the back door, climbed in at the wheel and looked behind him to make sure there was room to reverse.

Another three hours to go before everything was settled.

TWO

He was just over fifteen, for it was the year he took his certificate, when any thought of the Riviera first entered his universe, in a still sketchy form, but nonetheless more real than the tourist poster he used to see at the station when he went to La Roche-sur-Yon.

On that day he was far from guessing that, in a more or less indirect fashion, it was his destiny that was at stake.

Why he had accompanied his father to Luçon he was unable to recall. At all events this meant that it was a Thursday, since on other days, when he went there to school, he rode his bicycle.

Had he wanted to see a school friend and asked for a lift on the cart? That was possible, for it was raining hard and a strong sea wind made the hood flap. He could see again the large patches of damp on the flanks of the mare, her back covered with a strip of canvas.

They never talked much together, his father and he. They must have covered the five miles separating Champagné and Luçon in silence; a flat road, like the rest of the marshland, with every so often a one-story house, a *cabane* as it was called locally, in the meadows lapped by the sea.

The real landscape, there, was the sky, more vast than elsewhere, scarcely broken by the indentation of a church spire on the horizon, a sky so vast that houses, roads, cars, and, all the more, human beings appeared minute.

It was the sky which was alive, filling itself with heavy black clouds which would burst, or else with huge white ones, luminous and still, or again with fleecy wisps which would cluster together in reddish strips at sunset.

It had probably been raining all day, as so often happened. When there was no fair and no market at Champagné or in the neighboring parishes, the inn, except in the season, was to all intents and purposes empty.

It was his great-grandfather, a butcher by trade, who had started it and given it the name of the Ox and Crown, which was still written up on the sign in gold letters dating back a century. The ceiling was low, yellowed, almost brown, like the walls, the paneling, the tables on which the locals propped their elbows on Sundays, to drink their carafes of *muscadet* and play cards or dominoes.

They would still be wearing the black suits they had put on to go to Mass. During the week, as well, they were nearly always in black, because they were using up old Sunday suits.

And throughout the house there reigned a smell of wine dregs, alcohol, stale tobacco, with a not unpleasant mustiness in the bedrooms which remained for Émile the smell of the real countryside. It must have come from the beds, perpetually damp, with their sisal mattresses. Or did the smell come from the haystack at the back, in the meadow, for his father had a plot of land and two cows?

He had never been farther than La Roche-sur-Yon and Les Sables-d'Olonne to the north, La Rochelle to the south, Niort to the east.

He saw only local country folk, a few commercial travelers, the occasional lawyer lunching at the hotel and, in summer, tourists merely passing through.

He could not remember any real conversation with his father. As for his mother, she seemed to bear a grudge against him for being born six years after her two other children, when she was counting on not having any more.

Even as a small child he had not dared tell her, for example, that he had a stomach ache, as she would then look at him with the eye of somebody who knows better, somebody who is not to be deceived.

"You're just pretending to have a stomach ache because you haven't done your homework and you're afraid of going to school."

This had struck him forcibly. She used to reason in this way about everything. And as there was some truth in it since indeed he did not know his lesson, it had bothered him for a long time.

He had ended by finding out that he really did have a stomach ache—so he was not *pretending*—because he did not know his lesson and therefore because he was afraid.

As for his father, he did not trouble about such matters. He lived in a world of big personalities, men who talked about meadows, hay, heads of cattle, or local politics, over carafes of wine or glasses of liqueur.

Perhaps Émile had accompanied him that day only because it had been raining since morning, and he was bored in the house where he had never had any place to himself. His sister, Odile, who was twenty-two, had her own room. He slept in his brother Henri's room, an attic like Ada's, and he had nothing in common with Henri who, at twenty, was already the replica of his father.

Henri worked with a cattle dealer and would become a cattle dealer in his turn, which would not prevent him from taking over the Ox and Crown. It all went together.

It was not long before Odile married a tall fair-haired clerk from Luçon.

As for Émile, he would have to look after himself as best as he could.

That was more or less his situation at this period. He was smaller than the rest of the family, and while the others were tough and gnarled he was ashamed of the chubbiness of his body.

The cart had stopped first at the freight station, where his father loaded up with some sacks, probably of fertilizer. Then, not far from the Cathedral, while the rain was still falling in buckets, they had made a halt at the Three Bells.

"Out you get," his father had said.

The Three Bells deserved to be called a hotel because of its big white façade, its two dining rooms, the bathroom on each floor, and the coat of arms displayed at either side of the door, but it was also an inn where, on market days, the stables were full of horses, there were wagons in the yard, and more or less drunken peasants in the dining rooms and kitchen.

Louis Harnaud, called Big Louis, was a friend of his father's and passed for a rich man. His complexion was highly colored, almost violet, for he drank from morning to night, in his white uniform and chef's cap, with customers whom, had it been necessary, he would have gone out to find in the street.

"Good to see you, Honoré. . . . Have you brought the lad along? . . . Sit down, while I just go and fetch a bottle. . . ."

There was, as well, a cashier's desk in the hall, at which, on days when there was a crowd, the worthy Madame Harnaud would take her place with as much gravity as if she were ascending a throne.

Their daughter, Berthe, had gone to the same school as Émile, but being two years older, she had already passed her certificate. He had not seen her that day. Perhaps she had gone to her piano lesson?

The three of them were ensconced in a corner of the room where the set meal was served, and through the lace curtains Émile could see the rain falling, passers-by holding their umbrellas like shields.

"I was saying to my wife only yesterday that I wanted to talk to you. . . ."

Émile was used to these conversations, slow to get started, as if each mistrusted the other, and one might still have thought they were discussing the sale of a meadow or a cow.

"Do you like it at Champagné?"

His father, who did not know what was coming next, prudently said nothing.

"What about your elder boy?"

"He's doing all right. . . ."

"I gather your daughter's getting married?"

Everybody in the neighborhood knew about it. These then were just preliminary maneuvers, yet despite the apparent futility of the words, each one of them counted.

"If I thought of you straight away it was because I had the impression—though I may be wrong—that you were ambitious for your sons. . . ."

As he said this he was looking at Émile as if to enlist him as his accomplice.

"It never occurred to you to set yourself up in a more important place than Champagné?"

"It was good enough for my parents and grandparents. I suppose it's good enough for my children."

"Listen, Honoré . . ."

They had been at school together and both of them were innkeeper's sons.

"Anyway, here's to you!"

Just then Madame Harnaud had pushed open the door and, seeing the two men talking, had withdrawn without a sound.

"Mind you, I don't want to influence you. I'm going to say what I have in mind because I like you, and I know your worth. . . ."

He was taking a long, roundabout route before coming to the point.

"You must have heard that Madame Harnaud and I finally treated ourselves to a holiday. . . ."

He was not the only person to call his wife by her surname. Most of the local businessmen did the same.

"For years she's wanted to see the Riviera, and we went and spent three weeks in Nice. . . ."

He was tipping his chair back, his glass in his hand, a more sly look in his eye.

"You've never been there, have you?"

"Never."

"Perhaps it would be just as well if you never did."

That made him laugh.

"Do you know that in November, down there, you can go about without an overcoat and there are still enough tourists to fill half the hotels?"

When he finally got to the matter in hand, the bottle was empty and he went off to fetch another.

"I'm fifty-eight years of age, seven months younger than you are. See how well I remember? For some time now I've been thinking about retiring, as my liver and my kidneys are giving me trouble and the doctor says my way of life doesn't help matters. Wait a second. . . ."

He went out, came back with some postcards and photographs. "First, just have a glance at those. . . ."

There was a panorama of Nice, with the Baie des Anges in deep blue, other views of the town, of Antibes, Cannes, women in picturesque costume, their arms loaded with flowers, a little fishing port, probably Golfe-Juan, with nets drying along the jetty.

"Do you know what sort of people you meet mostly in Nice and around those parts? People like us, like you and me, who have drudged all their lives to put a bit of money aside and finally made up their minds to have a good time. That's what it is! I must say I began by wondering whether I wouldn't follow their example, buy a flat or a bungalow and retire there with my wife and daughter.

"Then I started looking at the advertisements. The place is full of agencies, as they call them, which rent and sell villas and businesses.

"Just look at that. . . ."

He spread out on the table some photographs ranging from those showing Provençal farmsteads to some of five-story blocks on the Promenade des Anglais.

"It took a chance visit to a little restaurant that had been recommended to me for me to catch on. The owner is a man of our age. I realized, from his accent, that he wasn't from those parts and he told me he came from the Dunkirk area. A fellow like us, in fact! One fine day he got fed up with working in a place where it rained half the year around. As he hadn't enough money to live off his investments, he took this small restaurant I was telling you about. He doesn't have to worry. Half the year he is to all intents and purposes on holiday, and in the morning he goes out fishing. . . ."

Big Louis was becoming excited, and finally he played his trump card, the photograph of an old farmhouse, somewhat dilapidated, flanked by two big olive trees and surrounded by a pine wood. Between the hills, on the horizon, could be caught the shimmer of the sea.

"It's mine, Honoré! Too bad if I've made a fool of myself, but I've bought that little lot and I'm going to build it up into something good. There's a fellow on the spot who isn't an architect but knows the business better than if he were one, who's busy drawing up the plans. There will be a restaurant, a bar, five bedrooms for tourists, and I will even be able to keep chickens and rabbits, not to mention that I've enough vines to make my own wine.

"I'm selling the Three Bells. I need hardly add that if you like the idea, I'll give you first refusal and you can have as long as you like to pay for it. . . .

"With two sons . . ."

Honoré Fayolle had limited himself to a nod of the head, without saying yes or no. In the end, after discussions in low voices in the inn at Champagné, it had been no.

Big Louis had duly sold the Three Bells to someone who had made enough money in a Paris bar and had dreamed of ending his days in a small provincial town.

The Harnauds, father, mother, and daughter, had left the district to set up house at La Bastide between Mouans-Sartoux and Pégomas.

In actual fact, this was the real beginning, in so far as a beginning exists.

For four years, Émile had heard no further mention of the Harnauds or of the Riviera.

After he had passed his certificate, his father had asked him:

"What are you planning to do?"

He had no idea, except that he had decided to leave Champagné.

"The owner of the Hôtel des Flots at Les Sables is looking for an apprentice kitchen-hand for the season."

He liked the vast beach at Les Sables-d'Olonne, the swarms of people from the far corners of France. He had scarcely been able to take advantage of it that summer, confined as he was for most of the time in the basement kitchen.

In October the proprietor had recommended him to a colleague in Paris, who kept a small restaurant near Les Halles, and he had worked there for two years. He had even followed, if somewhat erratically, a course in hotel management.

He was nineteen and was doing a season at Vichy when he received a letter from his father, which was a rare event. It was written in purple pencil, on writing paper sold in packets of six sheets with six envelopes at the grocery in Champagné.

"Your mother is well. She has hardly any more trouble with her rheumatics. Your brother is getting married, in the spring, to the Gillou girl, and they are both setting up house here. I'm just writing to tell you that Big Louis, who used to keep the Three Bells at Luçon, as I am sure you will remember, has had a stroke and is half paralyzed. He has started a good business near Cannes and his wife has let me know he would be pleased if you would like to go and work with them. Their daughter Berthe is not married. They have no son and they are in a difficult position. . . ."

A further link in the chain. He had read this letter in the huge kitchen of a big hotel at Vichy where there were fifteen of them, with napkins around their necks, caps on their heads, bustling around the ovens.

Was it, perhaps, the change which had attracted him? He did not like the chef, and the chef did not like him. He had left that very day, and on the next he first set eyes on La Bastide, which had become only a part of what it was now.

Big Louis, who was no longer big, but flaccid, with cheeks which hung like those of an old dog, was seated in a wheel-chair on the terrace and could utter only barely distinguishable grunts.

His wife, whose hair had turned white, made an attempt to appear delighted, but the moment she was no longer in her husband's presence began to cry.

"I'm so glad you've come, Émile! If only you knew how unhappy I have been down here! When I think that it was I who dreamed about it all my life and persuaded Louis to come and spend his holidays in Nice . . ."

As for Berthe, she was just as she was today, as calm, as secretive, as wanting in softness, and yet she was a pretty, fair-haired girl with a well-rounded figure.

From the first months everything had gone badly for the Harnauds at La Bastide. First of all the famous Van Camp, who had sold them the property and pretended to understand everything better than an architect, had made plans which, when the masons and carpenters tried to execute them, had turned out to be impossible.

He had not taken into account the slope of the ground, nor the distance from the well, nor the thickness of the existing walls, so that they had to undo part of what was already finished, dig a new well, change the position of the septic tank.

On the pretext that this was the Midi, Van Camp had not allowed for heating, and the very first winter they had been frozen up, in spite of having electric heaters on so that they blew the fuses.

Finally Big Louis had discovered, at Mouans-Sartoux, a *bistrot* where at every hour of the day he could find company, and he had switched over from white wine to *pastis*.

At this period Ada must have been about nine years old, and if she were already in the neighborhood, Émile had taken no more notice of her than of the other children he used to see sometimes on the roadside. Nor had he heard any mention of Pascali, who had, however, taken part at one stage in the building operations.

That the inn had been finished in spite of everything was almost a miracle, and, with Big Louis now incapacitated, there were only the two women left to look after it.

Big Louis had lived another two years, part of them in his bed, part in the downstairs room or on the terrace, and Émile eventually succeeded in understanding, as Madame Harnaud and Berthe did, the sounds he emitted.

It was Émile, at that time, who occupied the attic which had now become Ada's room, and there were already the same iron bed, several of the stains on the wall, but not the colored print of the Virgin Mary.

At first guests were rare. They had put up a board on the Route Napoléon, with an arrow indicating the way to the hotel. They also advertised in the Nice newspaper and in the folders handed out by the Tourist Bureau in Cannes.

On some days, however, there was not a soul to be seen. On Saturday evening, Émile would go by bicycle to Cannes or

Grasse, where he would have no difficulty in finding a girl to dance with.

Oddly enough it was about a month before Big Louis's death that, without any reason, business had begun to pick up. People from Cannes, doctors, lawyers, businessmen, started the habit of coming to lunch or dine in small groups at La Bastide. The idea spread, and on Sundays lunches reached the thirty, then the forty, mark.

Émile, in white cap, was kept busy in the kitchen where a certain Paola, an old woman from the neighborhood who was Madame Lavaud's predecessor, peeled the vegetables, prepared the fish, and washed the dishes, while Berthe supervised the tables.

Big Louis had died at the height of the season and they had scarcely had time to bury him. After talking of transporting the body to Luçon, Madame Harnaud had finally decided, to avoid complicating matters, to bury him in the cemetery at Mouans-Sartoux.

They had three residents, including a Swiss woman who had promised to return for a few months each year, and they could not submit them to the sight of a long period of mourning.

Without noticing it, Émile had become more or less the master of the house, and he had replaced his bicycle with a motorscooter, until such time as a truck could be afforded.

He had never made any advances to Berthe. It had never occurred to him. Perhaps because he had known her at school, and because she was two years older than he was, he looked upon her rather as an elder sister. Now he had never much liked his sister Odile, who was even more strict with him than his mother had been.

One day when he opened the bathroom door he had surprised Berthe stepping out of the bath, her body pink and dripping with water, and he had had the same feeling of embarrassment as when, on two or three occasions, he had seen his sister undressed.

He had felt no real desire or even wish for any of this, neither the Riviera nor Berthe. Chance had placed him in this house, which had become his, almost without his realizing it. Belonging to a different generation from Big Louis, he had adapted himself better and had discovered the market at Cannes, the fishing folk, the games of bowls; he had even acquired something of the local accent.

He had gradually changed the menus and the decoration.

And then, the first winter after her husband's death, Madame Harnaud began to drop increasingly transparent hints to him.

At first it had been:

"I shall never be able to get used to this country. . . ."

It was no matter that it rained less than in Vendée: the rain here upset her more than the rain in her own part of the world, and, from her chair in the window, she would stare stony-eyed at the sky.

The cold also seemed more insidious to her, and she complained of pains in her back, in her neck, in her legs.

Maubi was already at work on the vines, the kitchen garden, and the farmyard, for Big Louis had bought, with the house, a sizable piece of land.

"That man steals from us. Our fruit costs double what it does in the market. You'll see, Émile, as far as these people are concerned, we will never be anything but strangers good for fleecing. . . ."

She used to write a lot to one of her sisters who was a widow, at Luçon, and who lived with her daughter, still a spinster at forty. In her heart of hearts she dreamed of going to join the two women. She did not refer to it at this stage, but she was preparing the ground.

"If only I could sell La Bastide again!"

It was too soon to think of that. They had sunk too much money in it and the business was not firmly established enough to tempt amateurs, while through the agencies they would recover practically nothing.

Émile was beginning to recognize the pattern. Big Louis was not the only one to have let himself be lured. Hundreds, thousands of others like him, who, after an active, often hard life, hoped for semi-retirement, had yielded to the temptation of the Riviera and put all their savings into an inn, a restaurant, a café, or some kind of business or other.

Most of them brazened it out and pretended to be satisfied, but one could see them wandering, in the evening, along the Croisette or around the port, like perpetual strangers.

They did not belong to the district and yet they were not tourists either.

"If only," sighed Madame Harnaud, "Berthe could marry somebody in the trade!"

Berthe seemed to escape the torments of other young girls and had no adventures. As soon as she got a moment to herself she would read, alone in the corner, deaf to all that was being said around her.

It had taken some time. And it had required an attack of bronchitis, in the depths of January, when the *mistral* was blowing from morning till night, for Madame Harnaud to make up her mind to speak out more clearly.

"If I don't go back there," she groaned, "I feel in my bones that I shall follow my poor Louis, and it won't be long before I join him in the cemetery. When I think of him buried in a country which is not his own!"

She was forgetting that it was she who had decided on this.

"My sister insists that I should go and live with her. That's impossible so long as I'm not reassured about what will become of Berthe and La Bastide. . . ."

Émile, who had taken her meaning, was not enthusiastic. For weeks, he had turned a deaf ear, occasionally looking at the young girl furtively and wondering whether, all things considered, the game was worth the candle.

"You will have to get married one day, Émile. . . ."

The truth is that he had become attached to La Bastide, despite its air of a stage setting, and he was not averse to the sort of life he was leading. Could he ever again spend his days in the stifling atmosphere of the kitchen of a big restaurant or hotel?

Here, he was his own master. The customers were rather like friends. He enjoyed, two or three times a week, going to the market in Cannes, prowling among the fishermen just in from the sea, drinking a coffee or a glass of white wine with the market gardeners.

He was beginning to know the people of Mouans-Sartoux and Les Baraques by their first names, and often, in the afternoon, during the slack months, he would go and play bowls with them.

He felt vaguely that he was being overcome by a form of cowardice, and already he would not have had sufficient courage to live in a hard and gloomy place like Champagné, where one could expect the land to yield nothing easily, and one had to fight with it.

One evening when Madame Harnaud had retired to bed and he was alone downstairs with Berthe, he had sat down opposite her, and, for a moment, she had gone on reading or pretending to be reading.

"Has your mother spoken to you too?"

They had addressed one another familiarly ever since their school days, without its creating any intimacy between them.

"Don't take any notice of what my mother says. She only thinks of herself. She's always been like that."

He did not really know her well, even after three years spent in the same house, and he was trying to interpret her reactions.

"I think it would be better if we had a little talk about it."

"About what?"

She had still not let go of her book and he had the impression that she was moved.

"About your mother. You know better than I do that she won't stay here long. She dreams of nothing but Luçon. These days she writes to her sister three times a week. Have you read her letters?"

"No."

"Nor have I."

It was a difficult conversation, and at this point Berthe made as if to get up.

"There would be one way in which she could leave here and still not lose her money."

He was afraid she would take it the wrong way, for he had seen her stiffen.

"It's not for myself that I'm saying this, but for her. For you, too, perhaps."

"Nobody need bother about me."

"Do you dislike me?"

She had turned away her head and it was only then that he had suspected her of having been in love with him for a long time, at any rate of having made up her mind that he would belong to her.

All of a sudden he had felt a little moved by it all. He felt sorry for her. She was proud, he knew, and she was now in a false position.

He had never paid court to her. Nor had he ever felt the slightest emotion in her presence, as he sometimes felt with other women. The time he had seen her naked, he had withdrawn without a word and he had never mentioned it afterwards.

"Listen, Berthe . . ."

He reached out his hand across the table. It would have made it easier to talk if she had put hers out too, but she remained rigid on her chair on the defensive.

"I don't know if I would make a good husband. . . ."

"You chase all the girls."

"All boys do."

He was sure, now, of what he had just suspected, and it annoyed him a little; he asked himself whether he would not have preferred a refusal.

"We could give it a try, couldn't we?"

"Try what?"

"I am fond of you."

"Fond?"

He had stood up, because he felt it was necessary, and he did it for her sake, so that she would not be humiliated. Standing, he put an arm around her shoulders.

"Listen, Berthe . . ."

Finding nothing to say, he had leaned over to kiss her and had found tears on her cheeks.

It was their first kiss, their first real contact. When their lips parted, she had murmured:

"Don't say anything. . . ."

And she had gone and shut herself in her room.

That was how another phase of his life had begun. On the next day she was paler than usual, and, as she seemed to be ashamed, he had given her comforting glances, trying to instill a certain tenderness in his eyes.

Meeting her in the corridor, he had embraced her without her protesting, and an hour later he had been surprised to hear her singing like a happy woman.

Madame Harnaud must have understood, for she took to going

up to her room very early, leaving them alone. Berthe would read in the dining room, while he finished his work in the kitchen, then went around closing the shutters and doors. After a moment's hesitation, he went up behind her and took her in his arms.

He was disconcerted to find her a woman troubled by emotions, who seemed to expect something more than mere kisses from him. It was she, first, who seized Émile's hand and put it to her breast, and after several days this girl, whom he had believed to be unfeeling, was behaving like a real female.

The most embarrassing part was the mother's latent complicity. She could not have been unaware of what was going on. Émile was convinced that she was waiting for the irreparable damage to be done so as to be reassured concerning her own future.

Now the irreparable could not be achieved on the ground floor, where all the rooms were public ones. Émile had no pretext to go into Berthe's room, and she never went up to the attic either.

It was the period when they were converting some old stables, separated from the main part of the house, in order to put up two or three extra guests during the summer.

As with the rest of the building, they turned it into a typical Provençal place, too much so in fact, and it had already been christened the Cabin.

One went down a step, and the floor was made of large paving stones like those in old churches. Pascali, the mason, had built a rustic chimney and the windows had small old-fashioned panes, while the ceiling kept its open beams.

Wooden stairs, which looked rather like a ladder, led to an upper floor divided into two small rooms beneath the sloping roof.

Tourists enjoy this kind of place, unlike anything else, where they have the impression of being separated from other people. They could house a family with several children there, or young married couples on their honeymoons. On the ground floor the bed was replaced by a large divan covered with flowered cretonne.

It was in the Cabin that it happened. The alterations were not yet completely finished when Émile had taken to going there after lunch for his siesta.

He used to lie down for an hour, fully dressed, like most people round about, hearing only the clucking of the hens, from the direction of Maubi's shed, and nearer at hand, the cooing of the two pigeons.

One afternoon he had just lain down and was only half asleep when he became aware of the sun suddenly streaming in through the open door. Then semidarkness reigned again. With his eyes closed, he could sense a presence in the room.

Finally Berthe's voice had stammered:

"Émile . . ."

It was in March, he recalled. They were hurrying ahead with the alterations, so that everything would be ready for Easter, which more or less marks the beginning of the season.

He knew why she was there and, all things considered, it did not displease him.

He had sat up on the edge of the divan, while Berthe went on:

"I came to tell you that Mamma . . ."

He preferred not to hear the story which she had prepared, and to spare her a difficult moment.

"Come here."

"But . . ."

He had pulled her to him and forced her, without her offering much resistance, to lie beside him.

"Hush!"

"Émile . . ."

"Hush! . . . I'll go and tell your mother presently that it's yes. . . ."

Afterwards he had preferred to remain alone for a while in the Cabin, for he did not want her to see his rather gloomy expression. Berthe must not think he was disappointed.

Was he really? To tell the truth, he had felt no emotion at all, scarcely the pleasure he could get with any girl, and it had all happened with a kind of embarrassment which spoiled everything.

Berthe did not leave any impression on him to speak of. Nor, in those days, did she displease him either and he had as yet no reason to bear any grudge against her.

It was difficult to explain, and yet, since then, he had had time to think about it.

She was a stranger to him. But hadn't he made love many times, often with a certain exaltation, with girls whom he hadn't even known an hour before?

These ones became friends straight away. What they did together, they did for their mutual pleasure. There would come to be a lighthearted complicity between them.

Afterwards it was still possible to make jokes:

"You certainly wanted that, I must say!"

Or else:

"You're a strange one, aren't you!"

To which he always found something to answer back.

It was a game, which had no consequences. If some of them put on amorous airs, and sighed in a melancholy manner, he was not tempted to reassure them or to pay them compliments.

"You're pleased with yourself, aren't you? You're reckoning: another conquest!"

Why not? He was performing his function as a young male. His father had acted the same way in the past, and so had all the others, who spoke about it sometimes with avid smiles as they emptied their carafes in the smoky dining room at the inn.

With Berthe, who had put a wild ardor into her love-making, it had a mystic side, as if they were carrying out a ritual sacrifice together.

It was almost a drama that they had played between them; and when she had suddenly bitten his lip, he had had an intuitive sense of a threat.

It was too late. At La Bastide he did not immediately find her. Old Paola, who was peeling vegetables in the semidarkness of the kitchen, where she always kept the shutters closed, gave him an ironical look.

It was as if everybody knew already, as if everybody had been waiting for what had just taken place, as if everybody, in fact, had more or less participated.

Even before he uttered a word, Madame Harnaud, the moment they met, looked at him with gratitude in her eyes and he wondered if she were not going to open her arms to him.

"I've been meaning to tell you . . ." he began.

He heard Berthe's footsteps overhead, which was all that he needed to make his task more difficult.

"I think, if you still want to, you will be able to go to Luçon quite soon. . . ."

She made as if she did not understand, but her face was radiant.

"Berthe and I have decided . . ."

"Is it true?" she could not help crying.

"If you agree, we'll get married . . ."

"Kiss me, Émile. If only you knew how . . . how . . ."

She could say no more, for she was sobbing. Only a long time afterwards did she mutter:

"If my poor Louis could only know. . . ."

It was another beginning.

THREE

Would it have made any difference if they had had children, or if Émile had been older? The time had passed so quickly since he had left school that he still had dreams about it and even at times imagined he was on the playground.

Like most of his classmates, no doubt, he used to play a role when he was a child, more or less conscientiously, trying to show himself to the others as he would have liked to be. And the role he had chosen was that of a little tough guy, a cynical young thug who would not let himself be taken for a ride.

Yet now already, scarcely grown up, he was married, with a mother-in-law, responsibilities, a considerable business to manage.

He was not one to analyze himself for the pleasure of it, nor to look at himself in a glass. Nevertheless he sometimes had the sensation of floating, ill at ease, as if he were wearing clothes a size too big for him.

On these occasions he felt like a child of thirteen or fourteen whose voice is just beginning to break and who sticks on a false beard for the part of a knight, a king, or an old beggar in the school play.

The world was not real. His life did not seem clear-cut. On waking up in the morning he could have gone back to being the small boy who thought only of his lessons and his marbles, or the young apprentice sneaking a slice of ham when the chef had his back turned.

There was worse than that. But he did not like to admit it, even in his heart of hearts, for it was too disturbing: in the presence of Berthe he sometimes had the sense of being in the presence of his mother.

The reason was not a physical resemblance. He could not have said what were the characteristics common to the two women. Besides, he paid it as little attention as possible. It was a fugitive sensation, which he tried at once to shake off.

The way both of them had, for example, of looking at him, as if to read his thoughts, as if it were their right, their *duty* to see right through him.

"You will always tell me the truth, won't you?"

That was one of Berthe's remarks. A basis which she had established, unilaterally of course, for their relationship.

"I couldn't bear you to lie to me."

His mother used to say:

"No one's allowed to tell fibs to his mother."

She would add, sure of herself:

"Besides, even if you tried, you wouldn't succeed."

With Berthe, it was tacitly understood. She watched him. From morning until night, she held him as if at the end of a thread and, all of a sudden, when he thought he was alone, he would hear her asking a question.

"What are you thinking about?"

Why did he blush, even when he still had nothing to hide? He felt himself guilty before the event, reacted as he had done with his parents or at school, and it humiliated him, made him clench his fists.

It was at these moments, above all, that it would occur to him that Berthe had bought him. It was not entirely an empty notion. There had been a brief scene, with few words spoken, but which had nonetheless marked him for the rest of his life.

They had just chosen the date for their marriage: the week after Easter. If they waited any longer, in fact, they would have to put the ceremony off until the autumn, because of the summer season. Later, moreover, his own parents, busy, too, with their own inn, would not be able to come to the wedding, and Madame Harnaud insisted on their being there and that things should be done in the proper style.

For her, it was already a disappointment that the marriage would not be celebrated at Luçon, in the sight of all the people she knew.

The two women, he suspected, had a more important reason to hurry things. The mother knew as well as her daughter what had happened in the Cabin, and the one, like the other, was afraid lest Berthe should be too visibly pregnant on the day of her marriage. They did not yet know that there was no danger. And that was another question which would soon cause Émile further humiliation.

Perhaps, after all, they were not too sure of him and asked themselves whether, one fine morning, he might not vanish.

The fact remains that one Friday, a fortnight before the date fixed, Madame Harnaud did not go upstairs to bed in her usual way but remained downstairs with them. Having finished his work in the kitchen Émile had joined the mother and daughter in the dining room, where they would sit when there were no guests and where, since it was chilly, they had made a fire of two or three vinestocks.

He liked the smell of them. Something surprised him in the demeanor of Madame Harnaud, who to all appearances was knitting peacefully in her normal manner.

"Sit down with us for a minute, Émile."

In Vendée, and when he was only on the staff at La Bastide, she had used "*tu*" to address him, but instinctively, when he had become the only man in the house, she had taken to saying "*vous*."

"I was wondering if you had thought about the contract."

He did not understand immediately.

"What contract?"

"The marriage contract. When people do not sign a contract, it means they are marrying under the agreement to divide all their property equally. I don't know how you both feel about it, but . . ."

She didn't finish her sentence; the "but" sufficed to show what she had in mind.

It was then that Émile had noticed, on the table, a number of letters folded into four, which were not in the handwriting of

Madame Harnaud's sister. On the back, moreover, he managed to read a printed letterhead: Gérard Palud.

The name was familiar to him, as it used to be mentioned by his parents, who had had recourse on several occasions to this lawyer. For so he was called, although his profession was an ill-defined one. Not far from the Three Bells at Luçon he kept a grocery store with green-tinted windows where country people used to queue on market days.

Palud had worked a number of years as a notary's clerk, then had started a business on his own, advising clients about their transactions, whether buying or selling goods, about wills, investments, or inheritances. In a semiofficial capacity he also took care of their lawsuits, and he stood roughly in the same relation to real lawyers, real solicitors or notaries, as a bonesetter or healer does to doctors.

"I presume," Madame Harnaud went on after a silence, "that the two of you intend to draw up a marriage contract?"

It was then that Berthe had raised her head and looked at Émile with a look he was never to forget, before saying quietly, with a faint tremor of her lips:

"No."

The mother was taken in, imagined it to be generosity on the part of her daughter, or the blindness of love. The proof is that she had countered, not without a touch of irritation:

"I know what one feels when one is young. All the same, one must look a little further, for none of us can foresee the future."

Berthe had repeated firmly:

"We do not need a contract."

He could not have said by exactly what mechanism these words constituted a sort of act of possession of his person. Had not Berthe bought him, much more safely and surely than by any contract duly signed and sealed?

If she disdained any contract, it was because she was sure of herself and she relied only on herself to keep her husband.

"I don't want to insist. It's your affair between the two of you. If your poor father was alive, though, I think . . ."

"Did you have a marriage contract, you and he?"

"The case was not quite the same."

It was worse, since Madame Harnaud, born in a shack on the

marshes, had been a maid at the Three Bells Hotel before her marriage, and Big Louis had waited till she was four months pregnant before marrying her. Émile knew the facts very well since he now had the papers in his keeping.

"As far as La Bastide goes, and my share in it . . ."

She was withdrawing reluctantly from the positions prepared by herself and Palud, with whom, they discovered, she had exchanged a considerable number of letters over the past few weeks.

"I suppose you would like to take possession right away of your share of your father's inheritance?"

A closed, attentive expression on her face, Berthe listened, taking care not to answer too quickly.

"As far as La Bastide is concerned, I trust the two of you. Émile is intelligent, hard-working, and I have seen the way he manages things. So there is no reason why I should take my money out of it. . . ."

She had some idea in the back of her mind, which had perhaps been instilled there by Palud.

"As I am going to live in Luçon and, now that my poor husband is dead, I shall not last so very long . . ."

The way was tortuous, but she got there in the end.

"For you two it is a nuisance to have to render accounts to me each year. As for me, at my age . . ."

She was not saying that she had only a relative confidence in her son-in-law.

"The simplest thing, to avoid all discussion, is for you to pay me a remittance during my lifetime. In this way you are masters in your own house and I shall have no more to do with the business side. . . ."

It was not in fact true. Among the papers folded into four in front of her she picked out a draft agreement in Palud's handwriting. If the deed provided for an annual remittance amounting to well over half the present income from La Bastide it also reserved for Madame Harnaud, in the guise of a guarantee, a mortgage on the house, the grounds, and the business.

"I have been given the address of a notary in Cannes, and all we have to do is go and sign in his presence. . . ."

To all appearances Berthe had not had any hand in this transaction. She certainly had not been kept informed of the correspondence between her mother and the lawyer in Luçon. For her, the marriage itself was enough, without other documents.

It was, perhaps, partly love. Émile often came to think about it afterwards, and he would ask himself the question. He had scruples about blackening her character. He would be only too glad to allow that she had a kind of love for him. He even used to wonder whether it had not begun before his departure from Luçon, when she was only a child.

There exist girls like that who, the moment they become adolescents, decide that such and such a boy shall become their husband. It was a fact that she had not given herself to anyone else, that she had not gone about with other young men, and that when she had come to him in the Cabin she was a virgin.

But didn't Émile's mother love her son, too, *in her fashion*?

When the subject had been raised of a marriage contract designed, basically, to defend her against her husband, to safeguard her fortune, Berthe had said no, simply, firmly.

Was she hoping he would be grateful to her for it and see it as a gesture of generosity or blind love?

It turned out in precisely the opposite way. Émile had not protested, nor argued. He accepted. Chiefly because he had no say in the matter, because, up till now, he had in fact been nothing more than the employee of Big Louis, and then of the two women.

The roles, within the two couples, had been reversed. Big Louis had married his servant, after giving her a child.

His daughter was marrying their servant after giving herself to him.

So much the worse for Émile if he were making a mistake. At all events he was sincere: for him, there was no difference between the two cases.

And if the idea of going off, of leaving the mother and daughter there, entered his head for a second, he did not pay it much attention. Perhaps he had suspected for a long time that what did happen was the only logical solution.

La Bastide had become his personal possession. He had found it still unformed, incomplete, and it might have been thought then in danger of imminent collapse. Big Louis on his own, even without his illness, would probably have given up because, contrary to his expectation and hopes, he had not become acclimatized.

He was a man in exile, a man who had played the wrong card and who, in his heart of hearts, had perhaps been relieved to find himself delivered from his responsibilities by the stroke which left him paralyzed on all one side of his body.

Thus he had got out of it. It was up to Émile and the two women to make the best of things.

He had gone, almost without suffering, and his last gaze had fallen not upon his spouse, nor upon his daughter, but upon his employee.

God alone knew what that look meant. It was better not to think about it, not to try to guess the message which, perhaps, it contained.

So they had signed the documents drawn up by Palud, and the notary in the Rue des États-Unis had seemed surprised.

"Are you all three in agreement?"

This already constituted a kind of marriage, but a marriage of three, with Madame Harnaud saying "yes" first and bending forward at once to sign with the pen which was held out to her.

Next, Émile's father and mother had arrived from Champagné, the day before the wedding, the father in his black suit, the mother in a new dress of white flowers on a violet background.

Odile had not been able to come, as she was expecting a child any day. As for their brother Henri, he had to remain behind to look after the inn.

Madame Harnaud's sister and niece had made the journey, but three days earlier, so as to take the opportunity to see the Riviera, and the three women had gone to Grasse, Nice, and Monte Carlo by bus.

The wedding had taken place in the *mairie* and the church at Mouans-Sartoux. Many of the local inhabitants came to it, more with an air of being there out of curiosity than of taking part in the ceremony.

Though Émile had been virtually adopted by the locality, the others, including Berthe, remained strangers.

For business reasons, there had been no honeymoon. Quite simply, after the feast which went on late into the night, Émile and Berthe had gone upstairs into the bedroom once occupied by Big Louis and his wife.

"For my last two nights here I will have your room," Madame Harnaud had said to her daughter.

It was as striking as a transfer of power. They were henceforth to occupy the room of the grownups, the parents, with the walnut bed, the cupboard with the looking glass, the chest of drawers.

Émile, who had drunk too much—everybody had drunk too much, except Berthe—had tried, as he was undressing, to make a short speech to his wife. Wouldn't it be useful to settle their respective positions once and for all?

With the help of the wine and the liqueurs, he had imagined, during the evening, a kind of preliminary declaration.

"You've got what you wanted. Here we are married. From tonight onwards . . ."

He had thought up whole sentences, which appeared magnificent to him at the time, but which he had already forgotten.

There remained one thing he wanted to tell her, a declaration which he did not have the courage to make.

"Since we are married, I shall make love to you. But I had better admit to you right away that . . ."

One cannot say that to one's wife, not even to a girl one meets casually. It was nonetheless true. He felt no desire for her. He was obliged to make an effort. Was it his fault if, even though there was no resemblance between the two women, she made him think of his mother?

Fortunately the day had exhausted Berthe. She was strained, worn out. It was she who had murmured:

"Not tonight . . ."

This was a sign too: it was going to be for her to decide which nights he would make love to her and which nights they would go to bed without doing anything.

He was not unhappy. The proof is that next morning when he came downstairs ahead of everybody else and opened the kitchen shutters, he felt the same joy as on other days at looking at the countryside, the pale green of the two olive trees and the darker green of the pines in the sun, the golden shimmer of the water in the roadstead of La Napoule and the two pigeons cooing near the door.

They were not the same pigeons as they had now. The couples had succeeded one another, generation after generation. From time to time, instead of eating the young ones, they ate the old. The idea was for there always to be a couple to coo around the house, for it pleased the guests to see them caressing one another with their beaks and swelling their crops.

Madame Harnaud had decided to come and spend a month on the Riviera every year, preferably in the winter, when there were no guests and when, too, the weather at Luçon was at its most disagreeable. It was written into the agreement they had accepted, and if she had not thought of this precaution herself, Palud had taken it on her behalf.

Her first inspection, in November, had been of her daughter's belly. A short while later, alone with her, she had murmured, not without an unexpressed reproach:

"I was hoping to find you in an interesting condition."

This was to become an old refrain, an obsession. In all her letters there was a similar sentence:

". . . Above all, don't fail to write as soon as you have hopes in that direction. . . ."

The second winter there had been something like suspicion in the gaze she allowed to fall, no longer on her daughter, but on her son-in-law. And, toward the end of her stay, she had no longer been able to contain herself.

They were in the middle of a meal. It was still old Paola who was serving them. War had already been declared between her and Berthe, a veiled warfare, without respite, and it would not be long before one or other was the victor.

Berthe, of course! And it was true that Paola was dirty, that she had never taken a bath in her life, and that she spread around her an aroma of old skirts.

But it was also true that Paola was passionately attached to Émile, that for her he was the man, that there was no questioning his every deed or word, and that nothing Berthe said was of any importance.

If Berthe gave her an order, Paola would not reply yes nor no, would keep a tight face, as if carved in seasoned olive wood and, a little while later, would go and seek confirmation from Émile.

There would be other little wars of the kind to follow. Émile was resigned in advance.

He could feel then, in advance as well, just from the quiver of his mother-in-law's lips, that she was going to attack him.

Berthe had this same characteristic. When she was about to say something unpleasant, her face became quite expressionless, no doubt because she was keeping a hold on herself, but she could not stop her upper lip from trembling.

"Do you know, my children, I lately read an article in the newspaper which will interest you. I even cut it out for you. It's in my bag. I'll give it to you presently. . . ."

The article had not appeared in a newspaper, but in a popular weekly which dedicated two pages to horoscopes, two others to more or less new methods of healing, and the rest to film stars.

"In the old days, when a family was without children, it was considered always to be the fault of the wife. It seems this isn't correct, that it's more often because of the man. . . ."

The lip was quivering more than ever, the eyes were fixed upon the wineglass on the table, while the voice grew soft.

"Perhaps you should consult a doctor, Émile?"

He had said nothing, had simply turned a shade paler, his nostrils slightly pinched.

If he had an answer on the tip of his tongue, he swore to himself not to utter it:

"I would like to have a child from any girl in the street just to show you I am capable . . ."

The fact was that Berthe answered for him.

"I don't want any children, Mamma."

"You? What are you saying?"

"The truth. I am perfectly all right as I am."

She believed it, plainly. She had got everything she wanted. Not only did Émile belong to her, but La Bastide as well, and, if the guests did sometimes make mistakes, she was nonetheless the real mistress of the house.

That was the name, besides, which the local people gave her:

the mistress. They had not chosen the name at random. They were in the habit of watching people, especially outsiders, and they knew Émile, who played bowls with them on winter afternoons, well.

The second year he had bought a truck. Then Berthe had forced him to sack Paola, for she insisted that it should be he who spoke to her, who should seem to have taken the decision.

"If she stays in the house, I shall not come down from my room again."

When Émile had taken Paola aside, she had already understood.

"Don't you worry about me, my poor monsieur. I've been expecting it for a long time, and I'm ready to pack up my bits and pieces."

Berthe, who had put an advertisement in the newspaper, had chosen Madame Lavaud from among the applicants. Here was a clean body at last, one who had a certain air of dignity.

Was Berthe hoping that the new arrival would join forces with her instead of going over to Émile's camp?

For that was the point they had reached. It was not obvious. There was no open struggle, no declared sides.

What it was, was that nobody, either in the house or in the neighborhood, had adopted her. She remained an outsider. People were polite with her, too polite even: they showed her only too willingly an exaggerated respect and she was subtle enough to understand.

When the postman came in the morning, leaving his bicycle on the terrace, he would go and lean on the bar.

"How about it, Émile? Shall we make up a game tonight?"

If he caught sight of Berthe, he would take off his cap and appear ill at ease as he drank his glass of *rosé* which Émile had just poured for him.

It was nothing in itself, but it was the same with everybody.

"Is Émile in?"

"No. He's gone down to Cannes."

"It doesn't matter. I'll look in again later."

"Can't I give him a message?"

"Don't bother."

People knew his habits, knew where to find him. A kind of freemasonry was being created around Berthe, against her, which constantly opposed her.

"You haven't seen my husband?"

Instead of replying, people would look at her with an artificially innocent air as if they were trying not to give him away.

To avenge himself for Paola's departure, Émile had bought a little boat, a secondhand *pointu*. He had wanted one for a long time. For him it represented part of the Midi; it was the complement of La Bastide, of the games of bowls outside the post office at Mouans-Sartoux, of the Forville market and the little bar where he used to linger over a coffee or a glass of white wine.

The boat, however, from the moment he had bought it, looked like a challenge. He hadn't mentioned it in advance to his wife, had simply announced, one evening:

"I've bought a *pointu*."

He knew that at heart she felt the shock, even though she had enough self-control not to let it show.

"A new one?"

"Secondhand. It's in perfect order. I managed to get a complete set of fishing gear with it, including five lines for rainbow wrasse, two baskets for congers and one for bogues."

She did not ask him how much he had paid. Nor did she ask when he intended to go fishing.

In the height of the season he could not even think of it, as he had his hands full with work from the moment he woke up. In the winter months the sea was seldom calm enough, and in any case the fishing was not so good.

February, March, April, sometimes May were idle months, during which they seldom had more than two or three residents at a time, like the Belgians who were there now, with several guests passing through at midday and in the evening.

It was about the same in October and November, until the heavy rains which marked the beginning of winter.

Then he would get up as early as four o'clock in the morning, dress in the dark, and the idea never entered his head of planting a kiss on Berthe's forehead, where she lay pretending to be asleep. From the moment he put his hands to the steering wheel of the truck he became a free man, and he would drive down to the port whistling, to find, along the wharf, other fishing enthusiasts, nearly all of them older than himself, preparing their tackle and starting up their motors.

"Morning, Émile!"

"Morning, you old bastard!"

He had taken to quipping as they did, expressing a cruel truth sometimes beneath the guise of a joke.

"How's the mistress? Did she forget to lock you in last night?"

He got as good as he gave, naturally. Anyhow, it was the others who had started it.

He liked the throbbing of the motor, the silky sound of the water against the hull, the sight of the whitish furrow which widened in his wake, and it was a pleasure, later on, to lower the big stone which acted as an anchor, to break open the hermit crabs which he used as bait for catching *boulantin*.

He had familiarized himself with the colors of the fishes, so different from the ones he had sometimes caught at L'Aiguillon, in Vendée, when he was a boy. He had learned to detach the spiny hogfish from the hook or from the net, and to cut the heads off the morays, which had a nasty bite, with a single blow of his knife.

The sky would grow lighter, the boat rock in a world which seemed each time to be new, and little by little the air would grow warmer, the sun would rise over the horizon, Émile would take off his coat, at times his shirt as well.

Wasn't it worth the price he was paying? Sometimes he asked himself the question, only less brutally. Why couldn't he get rid of the feeling that he had been tricked?

He sensed, at the basis of their life together, God knows what treachery. As for Berthe, she had got what she wanted, had done exactly what she had set out to do, and he suspected old Mother Harnaud of having been her accomplice, just as Palud had been hers.

Even poor Big Louis, who was no longer with them, must already have had an idea in the back of his mind when he had written to him.

"You're as green as a newborn babe, Émile!"

It was not in connection with Berthe that they had said that to him, but at bowls, during the early stages. He had determined to become as good a player as the others, he who until then had never touched a bowling iron. At first, when it was his turn to bowl or set the jack, he would pull a face like a schoolboy who had just been asked a difficult question, and they laughed at him because he let the tip of his tongue stick out.

Then he would sometimes practice all alone on the terrace, in order to show them one day that he was as good as they were.

It was Dr. Chouard who, surprising him thus, had made the remark:

"You're as green as a newborn babe, Émile!"

As far as bowls was concerned, at all events, he had proved that that wasn't true, for he had become one of the best players in Mouans-Sartoux.

Sometimes Dr. Chouard would come and join in the game. He lived at Pégomas, in a dilapidated house, where Paola, when she had had to leave La Bastide, had found refuge.

The doctor was as untidy as his servant, his shirt always doubtfully clean, his tie, when he wore one, badly knotted, buttons missing from his jacket and even from his flies.

Like Émile, he had arrived one day as a fairly young man, from another part of the country, from the neighborhood of Nancy, and no doubt then he had had his ambitions. He had a wife, a wellkept house, the same one which now, from the outside, looked as if it were abandoned.

His wife was said to have gone off with an English tourist. But he had not waited for her departure before taking to drink and neglecting his practice.

For a certain number of years he had been the best bowls player and had been a member of the four which had won the Provence championship two years running.

His skill came back to him occasionally, by some miracle, since for some time now people had been unable to tell when he was drunk or when he was not.

Paola drank as well. Émile had caught her several times swigging straight from the bottle. He hadn't said anything to her. He had been careful not to mention it to Berthe.

For particular reasons, Émile had reserved an important role for Dr. Chouard in what was about to take place. It could even be said that, without Chouard, everything he had patiently been contriving for the past months would not hold together.

It was not for nothing that he had chosen a Sunday, nor that he had just made sure that Dr. Guérini was safely out at sea aboard his boat.

As for Ada, if she now at all gave the impression of playing a leading role in his life, she was in reality only an accessory, a secondary cause. But that nobody would believe.

The first time he had noticed her she must have been fourteen and she already wore a black cotton dress which might have passed for a school tunic.

He was following the twisty road down, in his truck, when he had seen her coming out of the pinewoods. He had wondered what she was doing there. He was not aware at the time that she was the daughter of Pascali, the old mason, and therefore that she lived on the far side of the pine forest.

He retained in his mind the picture of a scrawny, dark-skinned girl with long legs, hair like undergrowth, an animal expression.

He had seen her again several times and learned, at Mouans-Sartoux, various details about her father. Pascali, who was not a native of France, had come there young, and started work in the mountains, where there was a new road under construction then.

By a first wife, since dead, he had had two children, a boy and a girl, who were now approaching forty. The boy, who had become an engineer, lived at Clermont-Ferrand. The girl, so the story went, had turned out badly, and although there were few details to go on, some men claimed to have met her in Paris on her beat near the Bastille.

One fine day, Pascali, alone and already aging, had installed himself not far from Mouans-Sartoux, in an abandoned hut, and had begun working at his craft for people in the neighborhood.

Then, to everybody's amazement, he had bought a piece of land on the hill and had begun, in his spare time, to build himself a house.

He was never seen at the café. He did not play bowls, had no friends. He came to buy his own food and his daily bottle of wine, and everyone regarded him as a kind of savage; some even wondered whether he were not a little mad.

His house finished, he had disappeared for several days and returned with a woman twenty-five years younger than himself, who brought a small girl with her.

Since then, it was still he who did the shopping, the woman virtually never setting foot in the village. One day when the postman had a tax form to deliver, he had tried in vain to open the door. As he heard movements in the house, he had called:

"Francesca!"

She had finally replied with a grunt.

"Open the door, Francesca; I have a letter for your husband."

"Slip it under the door."

"Can't you open it?"

"I haven't got the key."

It was in this way that they learned that Pascali used sometimes to lock his wife in. As for the origin of the rumor that he had disfigured her on purpose, so as to make her ugly and discourage other men, that was more difficult.

Anyhow, before this same Pascali came to present his daughter as a servant at La Bastide, an incident involving a woman had served more or less as a trial of strength between Émile and Berthe.

There were eight residents in the house at the time, including two children from near Paris with their mother, who was the wife of a building contractor.

Had the guests noticed the game that went on?

An Englishwoman had stepped off the bus, at the bottom of the road, and had mounted the slope carrying her own luggage. She could have been equally twenty-five or thirty years old, or even thirty-five. As, bathed in sweat, she came up to the bar mounted on the wine presses, she had ordered in a somewhat hoarse voice:

"A double scotch!"

It was four o'clock in the afternoon and it was Émile behind the counter, in his white jacket. He could remember that it was very hot and he was not wearing his chef's cap. He remembered, too, the large circles of perspiration under the new arrival's arms.

"Do you have a room free?"

She had picked up a spoon to remove the ice which, out of habit, he had put into the whisky.

"For how long?"

"Till I get bored."

Might one not almost think Berthe had antennae of her own? She was busy doing her accounts at a small table near the window. From where she sat, she nonetheless called loudly:

"Don't forget, Émile, the last room is taken for Saturday."

It was not entirely correct. The truth was that on certain Saturdays, a lawyer from Nice, who was married, used to come and spend the night with his secretary. It was never definitely arranged. And when there was no room available at La Bastide, the couple had no trouble in finding one in some hotel or other on the Estérel.

"It hasn't been confirmed," he had replied.

And, to the newcomer:

"If you like I will show you the room."

Leading the way up the stairs, he had opened a door. The Englishwoman had scarcely glanced inside. On the contrary, she had asked, as though she guessed a good many other things besides:

"Is that your wife?"

FOUR

After twenty-four hours he still did not know whether he was attracted to her by physical desire or whether he was anxious to prove to her that he was not just the small boy she pretended to see in him.

She was called Nancy Moore, and according to her passport was thirty-two years old. She was really a journalist.

"I write stupid stories for stupid magazines in which wretched women try to find the path to happiness."

It was not so much the words which had struck him as the accent, not merely the English accent, but a disquieting blend of irony, cynicism, and passion.

He had had time, on the Riviera, to get to know her compatriots, both men and women, and he divided them into two categories. First, the ordinary tourists who come and spend a certain time on the Continent in search of the sun and the picturesque, to look at scenery and different human beings, to sample circumspectly various dishes they have heard mentioned and to leave again, more pleased with themselves than ever.

As for the others, he used a local term to describe them. He used to say they were the ones who had been "bitten." They were intoxicated by France or Italy, by a certain way of life, a certain easygoing philosophy, and these ones became more Southern than the Southerners, and in Italy more Italian than the Italians; they would not return to their homes except when it was strictly necessary, and some never went back.

There was one of them at Mougins, an extreme case, a boy of not more than thirty-five who some people said was the son of a lord. He lived the entire year round with his back bare to the sun and rain alike, hatless, with his ash-blond hair, which turned increasingly lighter, falling over the nape of his neck, and he let his beard grow; in winter he used to wear blue linen trousers, and in summer shorts of the same material; his shoes were *espadrilles,* or else he went about barefoot.

He painted. People came across him in vineyards, or at a turning in a footpath, with his easel, but this was probably no more than an alibi. He rarely went down into Cannes, was to be seen even less often on the Croisette, which did not prevent him from entertaining young men from all over the place and, as night fell, taking walks with them hand in hand.

Nancy Moore had almost as much disregard for her appearance as he had. Under her light cotton dress she wore no brassière and her breasts, which were heavy, sagged a little; one could see their tips moving and brushing against the material as she spoke. Her hair was unkempt, and she did not take the trouble to make up nor, when her face was shining with sweat, to put powder on it.

Nobody before her had ever looked at Émile with so much irony, nor with so much tenderness and avidity all at the same time.

She had at once fixed her daily routine. She spent a good part of her time on the terrace, writing in a large hand slanting not to the right, as with most people, but to the left. From time to time, indeed frequently, she would break off to hoist herself onto a bar stool, even at nine o'clock in the morning.

"Émile! I'm thirsty!"

She had not waited to become an habituée before calling him by his first name. She would change her drink according to the hour, now *vin rosé,* now *pastis,* and finally, especially in the evening, whisky, and her voice was always a little hoarse, her eyes glistening, without it ever being possible to say that she was actually drunk.

One could sense in her an ardent love of life, of people, animals, and things. He had seen her caressing, with sensuality, the gnarled trunk of one of the old olive trees on the terrace and she had done the same with the wine presses, their wood splitting beneath the varnish, which held up the bar.

"Are these real, Émile? How old are they?"

"At least two centuries. Perhaps three."

"So they've been used to provide wine for generations of men and women. . . ."

She would go into the kitchen to sample the smells, lift the covers of the pots, feel the fish and the poultry. She knew the different herbs and would rub them between her finger tips in the way that other women do with scent.

"What do you call those little monsters the color of corpses?"

"Calamaries."

"Those are the ones which spit out a cloud of ink when they are going to be caught, aren't they?"

He had shown her the little pocket containing the black liquid.

"With this ink I make the sauce. . . ."

She took notes which perhaps helped her articles. She always seemed to be defying him, brushing purposely against him, allowing her breasts to touch his arm; and when she leaned forward they were visible, naked and indecent, bronzed from her sunbathing, in the too ample opening of her dress.

"Your wife is older than you are, isn't she, Émile?"

Barely two years. It wasn't the difference in age which counted. What she meant to say was that Berthe was more grown up.

And Nancy was the most adult person he had ever met. Adult and free. Doing only exactly what she wanted. Accepting no rule and mocking the proprieties.

Between her and Berthe it was war, from the very first moment, and Berthe had turned a shade paler the first evening when they had heard a rumbling sound, at first inexplicable, from the Englishwoman's bedroom. Calmly, without permission or anybody's help, Nancy was busy moving around the furniture, the bed, the wardrobe, the chest of drawers, and next day, when they did the room, they had found the engravings which normally adorned the walls piled on top of the hanging cupboard.

At this period Émile was still under the impression that it was an affair between Nancy and himself. In the end, he had long afterwards discovered that in actual fact it had been an affair purely between Nancy and his wife, and the discovery had humiliated him.

In spite of the other guests—for all the rooms were occupied and there were quite a number of people in for meals—it was as if there were just the three of them in the performance, moving from the shade into the sun and from the sun into the shade, from one room into another and from the house onto the terrace, of a play almost without words, a sort of ballet of which the spectators did not know the plot.

Émile wanted Nancy with a desire which was at times painful, different from any previous experience of desire. When she was sitting at the bar opposite him, or when she came to seek him out in the kitchen, he sensed her smell, could imagine the sweat which, under her dress, ran in great drops over her naked body, leaving marks on the material.

She incited him, and in the way she looked at him she appeared to measure the strength of his lust, which made her laugh, a provocative laugh, as if to say:

"Dare you?"

The first morning, toward eleven o'clock, she had gone out on foot and not come back until lunchtime. He didn't know which direction she had taken.

"I spent a delicious morning sunbathing in the pine trees. I found a huge stone there. . . ."

"The Flat Stone."

That was the name of the rock on which she was by no means the first person to stretch out, more or less naked, to get bronzed by the sun.

"I don't know if anybody saw me. I heard people in the woods, children's voices. . . ."

Her eyes indicated the family having their meal in a corner of the terrace.

"Émile!" Berthe called.

She wanted him for something. She had wanted him for something constantly ever since Nancy had been at La Bastide.

"There doesn't seem to be enough *bouillabaisse* left."

It was a stifling day. Nancy, who disliked drinking alone, invited him to have a drink with her. And still he felt that shooting desire, as painful as a wound.

He had to show her that he was not a child, that he was not afraid of his wife. For three days this thought had obsessed him. When for some reason or other Nancy went up to her room during the course of the day, she seemed to be expecting him to follow her. He did not dare to do so, sure that a few seconds later Berthe would come and knock on the door on some pretext.

Nor did he dare arrange a meeting with her in the Cabin, where he had already adopted the habit of taking his siesta, since she would be seen entering it from the house.

She provoked him continually, with her lips moist, at times as though she were expecting him to throw her on her back in that very room, on the red tiles, beside the bar.

She had returned to the Flat Stone. At last, after three days of it, he had seized a basket from the kitchen, set off for Maubi's kitchen garden at an almost normal pace.

He did sometimes go there to fetch vegetables or herbs himself. More often, he entrusted this task to Maubi when the latter came, early in the morning, to ask for his orders.

He must not walk too fast, for he would have sworn that Berthe was following him with her eyes, from one window or another.

Fortunately the lower part of the kitchen garden was not visible from the house. It adjoined the pinewoods. By vaulting a low tumble-down wall, there were only a hundred yards of undergrowth to cross before reaching the rock.

Nancy, who could not but have heard him coming, had not made the slightest move to cover herself. Her clothes, her plaited straw bag lay beside her, and she wore dark sunglasses which prevented him from seeing her eyes.

He had had the impression of committing rape, awkwardly, clumsily.

He had never plunged with such animal passion into the warm flesh of a female before, and on account of those pupils whose expression escaped him, that mouth half open in a smile which he could not understand, he had raised his fist, at one moment, to strike her.

She had laughed, with a laugh which went on and on, while saying with that note of tenderness usually reserved for children:

"Émile . . . My clever little Émile! . . ."

It was she who all of a sudden had taken the initiative, who had played the man's role, triumphantly, to finish by murmuring, as she allowed her body to relax:

"Happy now?"

Somebody was calling, somewhere in the wood, not Berthe's voice, but Madame Lavaud's, and Nancy had once again put on her pitying smile.

"Off you go! . . . Your wife will be cross. . . ."

For appearance's sake Émile had been obliged to put a few vegetables in his basket. He walked with his head lowered. Her face and body looking cool in a light dress without a crease out of place, Berthe was busy writing in the shade, beside the bar.

"I think Madame Lavaud wants you for something."

Nothing was happening as he had expected. He was being allowed to reach the kitchen and get back into the rhythm of his routine. Then, a short while before lunch, Nancy came in, her straw bag in her hand, went up to the bar without anything happening.

"A drink, Émile! I'm dying of thirst!"

What was Émile afraid of? He reproached himself to find his hand trembling as he picked up the bottle of *pastis*.

"Have one too. On me."

Berthe had not even raised her head. On an impulse, Nancy stretched herself and said ecstatically:

"What a marvelous morning's sunbathing, Émile! Your wife ought to try it. She lives on the Riviera and she's as white as a Londoner!"

What place did this incident have in the whole picture? Was it a cause among other causes? Next day he was on the point of following Nancy. It seemed essential to him. It was almost an imperative. He had already collected the basket, from a dark corner of the kitchen where Madam Lavaud was drawing the fowls.

"No!" he had heard a voice saying.

It was his wife, of course, standing in the doorway. He had stammered:

"I'm just going to fetch some . . ."

"If you need anything from the kitchen garden Madame La-vaud will see to it."

Nothing else. He had not dared to insist. But he had not forgot-ten that humiliation, nor the one that followed the next day.

It was market day. Émile had thought it all out. By hurrying, he would reach the turning, on the slope of the road back, with time in hand to leave his car there for a while, to go and join Nancy at the Flat Stone.

He was so confident about it that before leaving he made a ren-dezvous with her in a glance. She had understood. They already looked at one another like lovers of long standing.

Gaily he had plunged into the bright commotion and the smells of the Forville market, called at the harbor, then the dairy, the butcher, doing without his usual coffee at Justin's.

The steep track was not wide enough for two cars. The truck was enough to block it. If a car came up or down, it would be obliged to hoot.

On foot, he ducked beneath the trees, caught the sound of chil-dren's voices somewhere, arrived panting at the Flat Stone, and found nobody there.

He was naïve enough to wait a good ten minutes, telling him-self that Nancy had perhaps been delayed, and he finally turned away to go back to his car, arrived soon afterwards in the hall where his wife was at her place, still making up the accounts, which was her share of the communal work.

She did not raise her head. He didn't question her. In the kitchen, it seemed to him that Madame Lavaud looked a little strange, but, as Berthe could hear them, he asked her nothing.

He would find out in the end. In a moment he would hear the voice of the Englishwoman clamoring for her *apéritif*. Time passed. The residents were sitting down to lunch. Berthe was see-ing to an Italian couple who wanted a table in the shade.

While the hors d'oeuvre was being served, he ran up to the first floor, taking the stairs four at a time, opened Nancy's door, and understood. Her suitcases were no longer there. The furniture had been put back into place, and the room had been turned out and aired so as to expel even her smell.

It was not until toward five o'clock, when Berthe had gone up-stairs to show some new guests to their room, that he had looked inquiringly at Madame Lavaud, and she had not misunderstood the unspoken question.

"Your wife threw her out."

That was all. He had never seen Nancy again. There remained only a somewhat confused memory. Three days, like days of fever, which he had lived without clearly knowing what was happening to him.

Yet those three days were to have their importance, rather like a scratch which turns septic.

He came to reflect more often than before:

"She has bought me."

For a month he had had no sexual relations with his wife, who, besides, had not insisted. Sometimes, seeing her head bent over their bills, he wondered whether she loved him, whether she felt anything toward him apart from a sense of ownership. This still troubled him. He would have liked to find an answer to the question. He would have liked above all to be able to tell himself she did not love him.

Everything would have become easier. He would have felt freer. Another six months elapsed, of life without incident, of daily routine, before Pascali appeared one morning in the kitchen doorway, with his daughter at his side.

"Is your wife in, Monsieur Émile?"

"She'll be down in a minute."

Berthe used to sleep late in the morning, had her breakfast sent up to her room and lingered over her toilet, no doubt realizing a girlhood dream.

Émile, who had recognized the young girl in black whom he had glimpsed occasionally in the pinewoods, had not wondered about this visit. To be more accurate, he had told himself that Berthe had called in the builder to do some repairs, for it was she who saw to that side of things.

He could still picture Pascali sitting in a corner, cap in hand, with his white hair which, in the gloom, gave him a kind of halo. The girl remained standing.

"Give him a glass of wine, Madame Lavaud."

It was autumn. The grape harvest was over and Émile was busy preparing a blackbird pâté. It was one of his specialties.

He had realized from the beginning that he must concentrate on local dishes and he had studied them with care. If his *bouillabaisse* was nothing out of the ordinary, since he did not always have the right fish to hand, and also because of the cost of making it, his calamary risotto, for instance, was famous among the gourmets of Cannes and Nice, who often made the trip, on Sundays, just to eat it.

His blackbird pâté was no less renowned, as was his stuffed baby rabbit, for which he refused to reveal the recipe.

Had not Nancy, who was very fond of her food, told him seriously and, he was convinced, without a trace of sarcasm:

"If you set yourself up in London, in Soho, you would make a fortune in no time."

He didn't want to live in London, but to stay here. He had taken root. He felt at home. If only there hadn't been Berthe . . .

She had come down in the end. He had called to her, from one room to the other:

"Pascali's here and wants to speak to you. . . ."

She had shown the mason into the sitting room and the girl had followed them in, walking in a way Émile only noticed now for the first time, the walk normally associated with Indians in Wild West novels, which is also found among gypsies who go about with bare feet. But she was wearing *espadrilles* and he noticed that her legs were dirty.

Without paying any attention to it, he could hear a murmur of voices. Then he saw Pascali going past in the sunlight of the terrace.

A moment later there were footsteps on the floor above, but half an hour elapsed before he found his wife by herself in the dining room.

"I didn't see Pascali's daughter leave."

"She's upstairs, arranging the attic which used to be a storeroom. I have taken her on as housemaid and that is to be her room."

He had had nothing to do with it. At first he attached no importance to it. He was pleased on the whole to have an extra pair of hands in the house, for Madame Lavaud couldn't do everything and custom was expanding.

"Has your husband seen a doctor?"

Time was passing, and what marked the passage of the years most of all was still the presence of Madame Harnaud in the house for about a month during the slack season.

She could not reconcile herself to the idea that her daughter had no children.

"You ought both of you to go and see one."

During the time she was at La Bastide she never ceased to spy on them, without seeming to do so, for to all appearances she was as discreet, as self-effacing as possible.

"Don't worry about me. You get on with what you have to do. I am quite used to being alone and I'm never bored."

She would knit for hours at a stretch, sometimes in one corner, sometimes in another, attentive to every sound, to voices, to the slightest whispers.

"Is she a local girl? I seem to have seen her somewhere before."

Ada, by now, wore a white apron over the shapeless black dress which she seemed to have adopted once and for all. For a certain time her hair had been the subject of almost daily dispute.

"Go and brush your hair, Ada."

Ada never answered, which exasperated Berthe. One could not even tell if she had been listening.

"Say, 'Yes, madam.' "

"Yes, madam."

"Well then, go and brush your hair."

She wore her hair falling over her neck, and it appeared never to have known the discipline of a comb. It was black, thick like the hair of Chinese women.

"Have you washed your hair as I asked you? Don't lie to me. If you haven't washed it by tomorrow, I shall put your head under the tap and soap it myself."

Madame Harnaud would say of Ada:

"Don't you think she's a bit mad?"

"It's possible. I don't know. Her father is a bit queer as well and her mother passes for an idiot."

"Aren't you afraid?"

"What of?"

"Those sort of people give me the creeps. I knew one like that, a young man who worked for your father, and one fine morning he had an epileptic fit in the middle of the kitchen. The foam dribbled from the corner of his mouth. . . ."

"I asked the doctor. . . ."

"Which one?"

"Chouard."

"He's a drunkard. I hope he isn't the one you call in when you are ill?"

"No. We see Guérini. Dr. Chouard looks in from time to time to have a carafe of wine."

"A bottle or two, you mean! I remember him. What does he think of her?"

"He says there's nothing wrong with her. Just that she is back-ward."

"Backward in what?"

"Some people, it seems, never grow up mentally past a certain age."

"What age has she stopped at?"

Berthe shrugged her shoulders. Ada had the advantage of not costing much. They did not give her money directly. They paid her wages to her father and he had asked that she should not be allowed any freedom. It was a convenient arrangement. She was always available, day and night, winter and summer alike, and only at distant intervals would she go off to pay a short visit to the house Pascali had built on the outskirts of Mouans-Sartoux.

It was Pascali who appeared on the terrace every two weeks or so and went into the kitchen, taking off his cap as he did so. He would sit down, always in the same corner, accept the traditional glass of wine, one only, never two, and remain there for half to three-quarters of an hour without anybody having to bother with him.

He asked no questions, did not kiss his daughter, did not speak to her except to say, each time:

"Good-by."

As for her, there were some guests who, the first few days, thought she was dumb. If she was not thorough and if she often forgot her orders, she nonetheless tried to do her job, and when she had nothing to do she even looked about for some way of making herself useful.

They had grown accustomed to her being there, more as one does to the presence of a domestic animal than to that of a human being. She made little noise. On busy days she did not sit down to eat, making do with scraps which she scavenged from plates and dishes returning to the kitchen.

Berthe had never insisted that Émile should go and see Guérini or any other doctor on the subject of her mother's insinuations. She had been to consult Guérini herself, one day when she had a sore throat. Had she mentioned the other matter?

It was possible. Émile did not bother his head about it. Since he had been living at La Bastide, he had never needed a doctor, and when he had had influenza, the fourth or fifth winter, he had cured himself with the help of grogs and aspirin.

Guérini and his wife came every now and then to eat at La Bastide, on evenings when their maid had time off. They were a pleasant young couple. People from Mouans-Sartoux were afraid they might lose their doctor, for they said he was far too intelligent to spend his life in a village, and that he would end up by taking a practice in Cannes or Nice, perhaps by going to Marseilles.

Orderly, conscientious, he had organized his life wisely. Whereas during the week he was on call at every hour of the day and night, to rich and poor alike, every Sunday, unless there was a storm, he reserved for himself a day of solitude at sea aboard his boat.

His wife, who understood this need of relaxation, did not accompany him, and stayed at home with their two children. The younger was only a few months old.

Was a man like that ever a prey to his own thoughts?

Truth to tell, throughout all this period, Émile had not felt unhappy. He had ended by adapting himself to reality. He no longer tried to decide who was master of the house, nor whether his wife treated him as a man should be treated.

Appearances were good enough for him and he, too, had his boat to which he escaped whenever possible. Apart from this, in the off season, he had his games of bowls, and on winter evenings people from Mouans-Sartoux would come up to play cards with him.

He did not wonder whether the others were different, nor whether he would have preferred another destiny. Life at La Bastide had gradually fallen into a routine fixed to the hour, almost to the minute. He always went downstairs at the same time, after hearing Ada go down first and get the coffee, and in the kitchen he would find Madame Lavaud, who had just arrived, knotting her apron.

Every room in the house was turned out in turn, and this indicated the rhythm of the days. There were, besides, the summer and the winter rites, which were quite distinct.

In summer, in July and August only, when they served as many as fifty people at each meal, Maubi's wife lent a hand in the morning and they engaged a waiter to help Ada serve at table, nearly always a young one, a beginner, so as to pay him less.

Sometimes they were obliged to change waiters two or three times during the course of the season, as there were some who stole or who drank, others who were rude to the customers or even to Berthe.

Thus, behind an apparently peaceful existence, there were constant little dramas, even though these might be nothing more than disputes with the tradesmen or the local workmen.

In actual fact it was Berthe who saw to all these matters, without ever a murmur. Apart from the marketing and cooking, Émile had no responsibilities and his wife hardly ever consulted him when there were repairs or alterations to be considered.

It was she again who made out the guests' bills, handled the cash, took it to the bank once a week.

Had he really wanted it to be like this? Hadn't he just let this situation develop through inertia? Had Berthe already become the enemy at this period?

He would have found it difficult to answer. At any rate his wife's body was more foreign to him after years of marriage than, for example, Nancy's, which he had possessed only once.

He knew two or three girls, in Cannes, whom he used to go and see every now and then, sometimes during market hours. He was sure to find them in bed then, because they used to hang about the Casino and the nightclubs, and, being short of time, he would make love to them hurriedly, rather as if he wanted to get his revenge, or to prove to himself that he was a man.

He did not drink, in the way his father-in-law had done all his life, or again in the way his father and brother still did, but made do with a few glasses of *vin rosé* during the day, especially in the morning around eleven o'clock, before the rush of lunch.

He didn't eat with his wife. She was served alone at a table either on the terrace or, if the weather did not allow it, in the dining room like the guests, at the same time as they.

The staff had their meals before anyone else, in the kitchen. As for him, it was only when they began serving the cheese and a dessert that he would sink into a chair, having cleared a space at the table, and swallow his meal in front of Madame Lavaud who was already busy washing up.

That was the routine in summer. The rest of the year, there were differences, and sometimes, in winter, especially when there was a strong *mistral* blowing, or when the east wind brought heavy rains, they went for more than a week at a stretch without a single visitor, a single person from outside, except for the postman, crossing the threshold of La Bastide.

As far as his plan was concerned, it was of no importance, for this plan was based entirely on the summer routine, or to be more precise, on the in-between season, already fairly busy, which came just before the rush of the summer holidays.

It was during the same season, two years before, that it had all started with Ada. After lunch, Berthe would go upstairs and lie down for an hour or two, like most of the residents. Shutters could be heard slamming all around the house at this hour, and it was the same with all the shutters in Mouans-Sartoux and the entire district.

Though Émile and his wife slept in the same bed at night, the famous bed of his parents-in-law, which Berthe must have regarded as a symbol, Émile had adopted, for his siesta, either the

Cabin, when it wasn't occupied, or a shady nook beneath a fig tree.

All this was not without good reason. To start with, he did not like undressing and dressing again in the middle of the day, and his wife insisted on getting in between the sheets. Further, their siestas did not last the same time. And lastly, he sweated freely, which Berthe disliked.

At all events, without the matter ever being discussed, he had won this period of liberty.

He would soon become drowsy, but he remained half conscious of what was happening around him, of the time, of the movement of the sun, and certain noises continued to reach him. Fragments of thoughts, no longer connected, passed through his head, becoming more and more shapeless, with sometimes pleasurable distortions.

Together with the time he spent out at sea, these were decidedly the best moments of his days.

Sometimes a desire would sweep over him, especially if he happened to recall Nancy and the Flat Stone, and he had caught himself stretching out his hand into space as if expecting to find a woman's body lying beside him.

It was a pity, that was all. It would have been agreeable. More precise images would come into his mind, and he generally ended with the consolation of promising himself to pay a visit next day to one of the girls in Cannes.

He had never thought about Ada. He scarcely noticed that she was a woman. Until the day when, during the afternoon, Berthe had taken the truck into town to make some purchases, some sheets and pillowcases; he could recall it quite clearly.

His siesta ended, he had gone back to the house and had found Madame Lavaud dozing in her chair, her chin on her chest. Intrigued at not seeing Ada, he had started up the stairs, calling for her softly. Receiving no answer, he had continued up the stairs and opened the attic door.

The shutters were closed. In the semidarkness Ada was asleep, naked on her bed, from which she had not drawn back the counterpane.

He had hesitated, not because of Berthe, but because of Pascali, who frightened him a little.

He did not want the man's daughter to maintain afterwards that he had taken her by force, or thanks to her being asleep, and, going over to the bed, he had said several times:

"Ada . . . Ada . . ."

He was sure she had heard him, but she did not stir, kept her eyes closed, her legs slightly parted.

Then he had touched her, at first with the tips of his fingers, and he had seen a tremor run through her.

"Ada . . ."

Her lips parted, she had sighed without speaking, but he would have sworn she had scarcely been able to repress a smile.

Anyhow! He had possessed her, suppressing all further reflection, and he had been startled at the radiant expression which had spread over the wild creature's face.

Never had he seen such ecstasy in another human being, and suddenly, clasping him frantically in her thin arms, pressing him to her breast with unexpected strength, she had stammered something which could only have meant:

"At last . . ."

Then, when, in his confusion, he would have liked to hold back his pleasure, she had begun to sob with happiness, with an interior joy, deep, welling up from within her, a painful joy, at once pure and troubled, the existence of which he had never suspected.

He just glimpsed her eyes. There were tears, big, childish tears, which had pressed apart the eyelids, and she had quickly closed them again, become motionless once more; then, when he stumbled to his feet, abashed and awkward, she had pulled a length of the counterpane over herself.

She was feigning sleep once again. Her small bosom rose in a regular rhythm, her hand remained clutching the rough cloth of the bedcover. One might have thought that nothing had happened, and he had left on tiptoe, closed her door without a sound before going downstairs and standing on the doorstep while Madame Lavaud began to stir in the kitchen.

FIVE

If it was still not the true beginning, that fortuitous event, which, in all sincerity, he had not expected, and which had lasted so short a time in comparison with the rest, was nonetheless to constitute a turning point.

Standing on the doorstep, he was invaded by a strange panic, largely of a physical nature, causing an unpleasant trembling of all his nerves. It reminded him, in a confused way, of the Bible, though he did not try to know exactly what: Adam and Eve realizing they were naked, or perhaps God the Father asking Cain what he had done with his brother, or perhaps, again, Lot's wife?

What had just taken place was no more serious than what took place every week between himself and other girls in Cannes or Grasse. His action had not been premeditated. Any man, in his place, would probably have behaved in the same way, and he was convinced that Ada had been waiting for him to act for a long time.

What was he afraid of? For he was afraid, with an undefined fear similar to that which seizes animals during storms and great cataclysms. He felt the need to go into the kitchen, to pour himself out a glass of wine, to be near somebody, even Madame Lavaud, whom he did not dare to look at straight away, but asked:

"My wife isn't back yet?"

He knew the answer. He would have heard the car.

"No, Monsieur Émile."

She was speaking in her normal voice. She didn't appear to know. And even if she had known? She was on his side. She used to glare balefully at Berthe when the latter had her back turned, Berthe who never lost an opportunity to humiliate her, as she humiliated everybody who came near her.

It was as if, in his panic, he was seeking a reassuring, plausible reason, and this went on for several days, during which he did not feel himself.

It was as if he carried around inside him the germ of something still unknown. People who are succumbing to an illness experience the same sort of discomfort and complain of feeling off-color.

His brief adventure with Nancy had had no consequences of this sort. On leaving the Flat Stone he had felt like singing, pleased with himself and with her. He felt he had won a victory, even if it had no future. He had shown his partner that he was not a child but a man, and that he was not afraid of a woman. Her body had satisfied him. It was a pleasant memory, warm and voluptuous.

And later, when he had not found the Englishwoman at their meeting place, when he had learned that Berthe had ordered her out of the house, he had clenched his fists in rage, knowing that he would never forgive his wife for it.

Nevertheless, he had not been disturbed in his innermost being.

This time, Berthe came back from town without looking at him with a questioning, let alone a suspicious, glance. Ada had gone back to her work, so like the Ada of other days that he might well have wondered whether anything had really happened.

For one instant this had been one of his fears. He did not really know her. He was well aware that, as he had heard people saying often, she was not like other girls.

Might she not have suddenly behaved differently, begun to look at him with love in her eyes, or with reproach, or even run off to her father's to tell him, weeping, what had happened?

Then as the hours, the days slipped by, he became more and more convinced that what he had done was necessary, and that what he would do from then on flowed naturally from it, as well as from a kind of fatality.

There had been several strange, tortured days, which he would not have wished not to live through, which were probably the most important days in his existence, but which left a chaotic and almost a shameful memory.

This, too, vaguely reminded him of his scripture lessons, of St. Peter betraying three times and the cock crowing.

In his bed the first evening, for example, beside Berthe asleep, whose warmth he could feel, he was annoyed with himself for having compromised, by an unpremeditated act, an equilibrium which suddenly seemed to have been satisfactory to him, a routine to which he had become so well adapted that he was frightened at the idea that it could be shattered.

It was almost certain that he would go on, either of his own accord, or because Ada would demand it.

Berthe would find out, sooner or later, Berthe, who knew everything that happened, not only in the house but in the village.

He was even more afraid of Pascali, who was not like other men, whose reactions were incalculable.

He pictured him arriving at La Bastide, not, this time, to sit in the kitchen and drink his glass of wine in silence, but to demand satisfaction.

Finally, he had taken no precautions and Ada was too ignorant to have taken any herself.

Supposing she were to have a child?

It was he who began to do the spying, puzzled at finding her as impassive as usual, with, at the very most, the reflection of an interior joy in her expression.

Perhaps after all he was wrong, and it was all a figment of his imagination? It was the fault of Berthe, of her oppressive presence, of the insidious way she had imprisoned him in an invisible but real circle.

He wanted to revolt and did not dare. He was so helpless that at certain moments it was Ada whom he accused of disrupting what he now termed his tranquillity.

"I won't go on with it!"

Five days later, he no longer kept to his resolve. His mood had changed. Alone in the Cabin, during the siesta hour, he thought about Ada in a piercing, painful way.

"In a while, when my wife has gone to lie down, come and see me."

It humiliated him to hide, to whisper behind doors, to wait like a young man in love for the first time, for a flicker of the wild creature's eyelids.

"Do you understand? Pretend you are getting some wood."

They burned wood in the kitchen range, and the firewood happened to be kept behind the Cabin.

As he waited for her he found himself hoping that she would not come. But she came. And he threw himself upon her like a starving man upon a loaf of bread.

"You must come every time I ask you. Will you come?"

Amazed at the question, she said yes. It seemed so obvious to her!

She did not understand his nervousness, his feverishness. He took her, one might have thought, as if he hated her and strove to destroy her.

It was days, weeks, before he recovered a certain equilibrium, which bore no resemblance to what he had known before. Émile was getting used to it. His fear was dissipating. He no longer thought of Pascali, nor of a possible pregnancy.

Life continued, with the seasons marking its successive stages and their rhythm, the season of mimosas, then of oranges and jasmine, the season of cherries, that of peaches, and, finally, before the calm of the winter, the olive and wine harvest.

They had several vines, which Maubi looked after. As the old wine press had been demolished to make room for the dining room, they sold the grapes to a neighbor, who paid with wine from the year before.

On the sea, as well, the seasons alternated, and he fished in succession for rainbow-wrasse, mackerel, bogue, and gilthead.

To his surprise almost two years had passed in this fashion, and he no longer needed to speak to Ada, a lowering of the eyelids was sufficient, to which she gave no answer but a gleam in her eyes.

Nobody, apart from himself, noticed that she had become a woman, that she had lost her stiffness and her angles, that her carriage was more supple, marked with a curious dignity.

Although she remained as secretive, as wild in her bearing, there emanated from her a serenity which he could only compare with that of a happy animal. Wasn't it rather in the manner of an animal that she loved him? Nothing else counted for her but to live in his wake, and the moment he made a sign to her, she would come running to bury herself in his arms.

She was at once his pet dog and his slave. She did not judge him, did not try to understand him or guess what he was thinking. She had adopted him as master, just as a stray dog, for no apparent reason, attaches itself to the heels of a passer-by.

A miracle was happening. Berthe-the-know-all did not dream of keeping watch on them, because of that very same pride which made her so fiercely jealous of all other women.

The idea never occurred to her that Émile could so much as look upon this creature as a woman, whom she regarded as half-baked, this slut, this scrawny savage girl, regarded by all and sundry as mentally arrested.

Thus, between Émile and his wife, an apparent peace had been established. He had fewer stirrings of rebellion. A little of Ada's serenity was spreading to him and he sometimes had to stop himself from singing, from seeming too happy, for fear he should be questioned about the reason for his joy.

Every now and then, at long intervals, from duty and from prudence, he would make love to Berthe, but despite himself, he would turn his face away when she sought to kiss him on the mouth.

He refused to think where it was all leading. And in January he had such an unhoped-for week that he did not really believe it until Berthe was on the train.

Madame Harnaud, who had come as usual to spend a month on the Riviera early in the winter, was now ill with pneumonia back there, at Luçon. Berthe could not avoid going to see her. As she packed her suitcase she was pale, less because her mother's health worried her than because her husband was going to stay behind on his own.

On this occasion she had said something revealing, not without having hesitated a long time beforehand. They were both in the bedroom, where she was finishing putting her underclothes into her suitcase. He had noticed that her lip was starting to tremble as it always did when she was preparing to say something disagreeable.

"I know that you're going to take advantage of my absence, but I must ask you to swear . . ."

"Swear how?" he had pretended to joke.

She was not joking, however. Her expression was serious and hard.

"Swear to me that no other woman will sleep in this bed."

Why had he been unable to stop himself from blushing?

"Swear!"

"I swear."

"On the head of your parents."

"On the head of my parents."

On the way down to Cannes, she seemed to be almost ill, and at the station she had turned her head away several times when they were waiting for the train. She had not waved. He had watched the outline of her face, blurred by the compartment window, to the last.

On the way home he had not yet made any decision. There were no residents in the house. Nobody was sleeping in, apart from Ada and himself.

When he got back, past nine o'clock in the evening, Ada was already in her room.

He had mounted the stairs, three at a time, feeling overexcited rather than out of breath.

"Come on . . ."

She had understood and shown a certain fear.

"Come on, quickly!"

For the first time, they were going to be together at last in a real

72

bed, without being afraid, without starting at the slightest sound, and fall asleep beside one another.

Was it not worth breaking his oath for this?

Madame Harnaud had recovered. Berthe had returned, taken up her place once again at the head of the household, and life had continued in its habitual rhythm.

Some Swiss women had arrived as guests, three together, for in the clientele, too, there were different successive seasons. In winter, for example, and in the beginning of spring, they never had more than two or three people at a time, nearly always women of a certain age, widows or spinsters, who came from Switzerland, Belgium, or the northern *départements* of France.

Then, over Easter, the families which only came for a short stay began to turn up, and there was a further relative calm until May.

Sundays brought Italians in cars, couples mostly, who mixed on the terrace with the local clientele, until the full holiday season.

Sometimes several days would elapse without Ada's being able to join Émile in the Cabin. Other weeks, she came to him two or three days running, and he had not cured himself of a ticklish anxiety which would lodge in his chest the moment he had given her the signal, while he was waiting for her, while he listened for her furtive step, and then while she was with him.

He had other periods of alarm, each month, for he continued to take no precautions, out of defiance, perhaps also out of respect for her and for himself.

They had never had any serious qualms, and though this relieved him each time, it was not without its worrying aspect, reminding him of what his mother-in-law had said about impotence in certain men. He rejected these ideas with impatience, refusing to admit that Madame Harnaud could be right, wondering whether at times his wife didn't have the same suspicion.

Wasn't it strange that she never made any reference to eventual motherhood, as if it stood to reason that they were destined not to have children?

The big scene occurred in June. He had drunk, in the morning, two or three more glasses of wine than usual, because Dr.

Chouard had called and he had kept him company at the bar for a considerable while.

It was on these occasions that he wanted Ada most, and he had given her the signal. The scorching air vibrated with the song of crickets, and the sea, in the distance, was motionless, with gray-green reflections like a sheet of cast iron.

Ada had come and slid up against him on the divan. He had decided long since that, if anybody disturbed them, she was to dash up to the first floor and stay there motionless, that if the worst came to the worst, she was to jump out of the window, which wasn't very high.

She did not have a chance. The door was locked, the shutters closed, but the windows remained open, creating a draft without which they would have suffocated. Émile had always been convinced that the shutters could not be opened from the outside and he gave a start when he suddenly saw the sun streaming into the room as violently as water surging through a broken dam.

Berthe cut a motionless silhouette in the rectangle of light, and the flood of sunshine following immediately on the semi-darkness prevented Émile from making out her features, or taking in the expression on her face.

Ada was already on her feet, had picked up her dress and was looking hesitantly at the staircase.

He heard himself say:

"Stay here."

Berthe still did not move. She was waiting. He got up slowly, ran his fingers through his hair and finally strode over to the door.

Without a word the two of them headed not for the house, but for the pinewoods which were not far off, and where a footpath began, the one which, like the path from the kitchen garden, came out at the Flat Stone.

So long as they were in the sun, which dulled their senses, they remained silent, and it was Émile who first, once in the shade of the pines, could no longer hold his peace.

"Well, now you know," he said, without looking at her.

She was not crying, did not seem to be on the point of an outburst. There was no hint of impending violence.

"All things considered," he went on, almost lightly, "it's better that way."

"Who for?"

"For everybody."

He felt he was being clumsy, but he could find no other attitude to adopt. It was true that he was relieved. Things could not go on indefinitely as they were.

"Still, I would never have believed that of you."

She seemed perplexed, overwhelmed. Had she, perhaps, had no inkling of the truth right up to the last minute, and only stumbled across it by chance?

"That girl does not stay in the house another hour."

He felt, all of a sudden, almost happy. He had feared tears, despair, reproaches. A hundred times he had been tempted to believe that Berthe loved him in her way, and the idea of making her suffer used to upset him.

Yet it was of Ada that she was thinking, with her voice full of cold rancor, like venom.

"Yes, she does!" he replied without thinking, or asking himself what his decision would lead to.

"What do you mean?"

"Simply that if she goes, I go with her."

Berthe's astonishment was so great that she stopped, rooted to the spot, staring at him with eyes which no longer understood.

"You would leave me for that half-wit?"

"Without hesitation."

"Do you love her?"

"I don't know about that, but I won't allow her to be thrown out."

"Listen, Émile. You had better think things over. For the moment you are out of your senses."

"My mind is made up. I shall not change it."

"And if it were I who left?"

"I should let you go."

"Do you hate me?"

"No. I don't think so."

"Émile!"

In the end she had come to tears, but too late, and they could no longer move Émile.

"Do you realize what you are doing? You are destroying everything, soiling everything. . . ."

"Soiling what?"

"Us! You and me! And all because a vicious child has got it into her head to take my place."

"She is taking nobody's place."

The words didn't express his exact thoughts, but on the spur of the moment he could find no others. Similarly, in a fight, one does not always strike where one intends to strike.

"And if I told Pascali everything?"

He looked at her, a hard look, with his teeth clenched, for she had found a threat which carried weight.

"I should leave just the same."

"Without her?"

"With or without her."

"You would abandon La Bastide?"

Viciously, she was casting about for arguments to wound him. She sneered:

"Would you get yourself a job again as a hotel cook?"

"Why not?"

Something was slipping somewhere. There was no longer any point of contact.

"Think carefully, Émile."

"No."

"And if I killed myself?"

"I should be a widower."

"Would you marry her?"

He preferred not to reply. Already he regretted his unintended cruelty. It was Berthe who had started it. He had felt no tremor in her which could be attributed to love.

Nothing but disappointment, the fury of outraged ownership. They were walking in silence now, and when they crossed a patch of sunlight, some grasshoppers chirped at their feet.

"You're sure you don't want to wait until tomorrow?"

"I'm sure."

He was obdurate. Even as a small boy his mother used to claim that sometimes he made people want to give him a good slap on account of his pigheadedness.

They covered another hundred yards without a word.

"There is one thing, at least, which I have the right to insist on."

"What is that?"

"For the others, even for Madame Lavaud and the Maubis, there must be no change."

He was not sure he had understood.

"We shall go on living to all appearances as we have done in the past, and we shall continue to share the same bedroom."

He just stopped himself from putting in:

"And the same bed?"

But he didn't want to take too much advantage of her.

"As for this girl, she has ceased to exist as far as I am concerned, and I shall not address another word to her except to give her essential orders."

He had to restrain a smile of contentment. After all, it was a victory he had won, thanks to Berthe's pride.

"Your dirty little tricks have nothing to do with me, but I don't want everybody to know about them, and if you're lucky enough to give her a child, I forbid you to recognize it."

He had never considered the problem from this angle and he knew nothing of the law.

"Is that settled?"

They had come to a halt, face to face, and this time they were now definitely nothing more to each other than strangers.

Was Berthe tempted, as he feared for a few seconds, to throw herself into his arms?

"It's settled!" he said quietly.

Without waiting for her, he headed with long strides toward La Bastide, and in the kitchen doorway found Ada helping Madame Lavaud to peel potatoes as if nothing had happened.

He simply gave her a wink, to let her know that everything was all right.

He was satisfied and bewildered. In a ridiculously short time everything had changed, and yet life was going to go on as it had in the past. He didn't know yet how he would face it. He had never asked himself whether he loved Ada, nor with what sort of love, and he was still incapable of answering the question.

For the moment, she was only playing a subsidiary role in the drama. What counted was the rupture between Berthe and himself, a rupture accepted on both sides.

If, a few hours before, they were still husband and wife, they were from now onwards no more than strangers, colleagues to be more accurate, for there remained La Bastide, and it was doubtless on account of this that Berthe had proposed her strange *status quo*.

La Bastide held them both, love or no love, hate or no hate.

Berthe had bought him, just as Big Louis had bought the old farmhouse, he was more acutely aware of it than ever, and she had just dictated her terms.

He went to play bowls at Mouans-Sartoux. The hardest thing, that night, was undressing in front of her, for it seemed suddenly indecent to show her his naked body. Nor did he know whether he ought to say good night to her or not. He avoided her gaze, slipped in between the sheets, keeping to the extreme edge of the bed.

It was she who switched out the light and said:

"Good night, Émile."

He made an effort.

"Good night."

Was he going to have to go to bed, each night for the rest of his life, under the same conditions?

Next morning, he went downstairs a few minutes earlier than usual, so as to be there before the arrival of Madame Lavaud.

"What did she say?"

"You're staying."

"Isn't she giving me the sack?"

Ada did not realize that this was acknowledging that Berthe was the real mistress of the house and that Émile had no say in the matter.

"No."

A silence. She did not understand. Perhaps she did not try to understand? Yet she wanted to know where they stood.

"And us?"

"Nothing is changed."

They caught the sound, still fairly far off, in the roadway, of Madame Lavaud's footsteps.

"I wonder whether I'll still be able to, now that she knows."

Instantly he stiffened and, without any precise reason, almost slapped her in the face, rapped in a dry voice:

"You will do what I tell you to do."

"Yes."

"Get the coffee."

"All right."

He did not ask her to come to him that day, for decency's sake, perhaps out of tact. He pretended to take no notice of Berthe, who affected the gestures of an automaton and only addressed him, in a neutral voice, about serving the customers.

After his siesta, he took the truck and went into Cannes to see a girl, the first one he could find, in order to calm his nerves, and, by an ironical twist, he knocked at three doors before he found one at home.

"Whatever's the matter with you?"

"Nothing."

"Been fighting with the wife?"

"Get undressed and shut up."

On these occasions, he gave the impression of a petty cad, a thug of the kind one sees playing the tough guy in bars. A sentence was taking shape in his head, to which he did not yet attach any meaning, and he did not foresee that it was to become an obsession.

"I shall kill her!"

For now he hated her, not just for this or that reason, but for everything.

He no longer told himself that she had bought him, that there was nothing in her but pride and peasant rapaciousness.

He did not even dwell any longer on her attitude the day before, nor on the bargain she had proposed to him, or rather the conditions she had dictated.

The matter had gone beyond the stages of reason and sentiment. The sentence surged up from his subconscious, like something self-evident, an indisputable necessity.

"*I shall kill her.*"

He did not believe it, was not sketching any plans, did not feel himself to be a potential murderer.

"You're kind of queer today," his partner remarked. "Anyone would think you were looking for someone to pick a fight with. I'll be all covered with bruises later on the beach."

He had to go home, because of the guests' dinner. He was a little anxious, as he went into the kitchen, for he was wondering whether Berthe had kept her word. Had she just said what she had, the evening before, to quieten him, and had she taken advantage of his absence to chase Ada out of the house?

Ada was there. Berthe was busy with her accounts. She was in her element. She would have been more lost if she had been deprived of her cashier's desk than of her husband.

Had her mother been unhappy, since the death of Big Louis? She had gone back to her sister and her niece, into their spinster world, as a fish drawn for a moment from the water would return wriggling to its own element.

It made little difference if he were being unjust.

"*I shall kill her!*"

This time, he said it to himself in front of her, looking at her, with her head bent over her papers, and it was already more serious.

No fiber in him trembled, nor pity, nor feeling of any kind.

Once again, it was not a project, nor even a resolve. It remained vague, outside the realm of consciousness.

He was not living, at the moment, in a solid world, but in a kind of luminous mist where objects and people were perhaps nothing but illusions.

He went and helped himself to a drink at the bar, a few paces away from his wife. For she was still his wife. Usually, as soon as he picked up a bottle, she would raise her head to see what he was drinking, and to murmur, when she deemed it necessary:

"That's enough, Émile."

He was waiting for it. Did she still dare to say it? Was it still her business?

Deliberately he emptied his glass at a gulp, poured out another, as if he were hoping that she would stop him.

If she had any urge of the sort, she suppressed it and continued to concentrate on her sums as if she were unaware of his presence.

So it was established once and for all: he was free!

On condition that he went on sleeping in the same room, in the same bed as she did, and hid himself away to make love with Ada.

He threw his glass to the floor before going off into the kitchen with a sneer.

Free, eh?

SIX

He still had a disturbed, incoherent phase to pass through, with his head in a turmoil. The season was at its height, all the bedrooms, all the tables on the terrace were occupied, and often the last to arrive had to wait at the bar for others to finish eating before they could get a place.

Apart from the waiter Berthe had sent for from Lyons, called Jean-Claude, who was too blond and rolled his hips like a woman, they had had to hire a local youth, with thick hair and black fingernails, and Maubi came in to lend a hand as well.

In the kitchen Émile would from time to time pick up a cloth to wipe his brow, so covered with sweat that after a while he couldn't see properly, and the pauses between getting each meal became shorter and shorter. There was no question of going out in his boat, or of playing bowls, and it was through all this activity that he used to think, when he found time, about his personal affairs.

As one of his colleagues in the basement kitchen of the grand Vichy hotel used to say, the machine must be fed. There, one might have thought one was in a factory. Instead of stoking the furnace of a locomotive with coal, they were ceaselessly filling the service elevator for the *maîtres d'hôtel* and the headwaiters upstairs standing ready to hurry over to the tables.

He felt that Madame Lavaud was watching him, quickly noting each new sign of nervousness he showed.

Everybody, inevitably, had noticed that Berthe and he no longer addressed one another except for essential remarks, in a flat voice, which, to himself, he used to call a cardboard voice. Were they not wearing cardboard masks over their faces as well?

What was stopping him from being satisfied? Almost every afternoon, even when he did not desire her, he would give the signal to Ada. She joined him in the Cabin and, automatically, because it was for this that he had asked her in the first place, she began by removing her dress.

"Lie down."

He had read that the larger apes huddle against one another to sleep, sometimes in entire families, without distinction of sex, and it could not be for warmth, since they lived in the heart of Africa. Was it to reassure themselves? Or through need of contact?

In captivity, when people tried to separate them for the night, they would become frantic, and in this book which had fallen into his hands, it was claimed that some of them pined away and died.

Sullenly, fiercely, he clung to Ada, his hand upon her shoulder, her back, her stomach, no matter where, and he tried to make himself sleep while she lay still with her breathing almost suspended.

Something was disturbing him, and he would ask himself questions to which he could not or did not want to find satisfactory answers.

Supposing things had taken a different turn and, against all likelihood, Berthe had left, for example, thus giving him back his liberty; would he have married Ada?

The answer ought to have come to him clearly, and yet this was not the case. He even asked himself sometimes whether he loved her, and the very fact of posing the question made him angry with himself.

Ada did not judge him, did not spy on him to correct him, to make him into what she would have wished him to be. If she was attentive to his actions and behavior, to his expression, the curl of his lip, it was to divine his wishes and to do everything that lay in her power to make him happy.

Was he sure, on his side, that he looked upon her altogether as a human being? He had nothing to say to her, remained content with caressing her, and for her, as for an animal, it was enough.

He would never leave her, for he needed her, especially at present. Berthe had, knowingly, put the two of them in a position at once painful and ridiculous.

They were not allowed to leave. They could touch one another only in private, even though everybody was certainly aware of what was going on. In front of other people, he was not even allowed to look at her.

He was a prisoner, like a May bug on the end of a line, and it was Berthe, with her appearance of melancholy dignity, who held the other end of the line.

It was again a religious term which came back to him, despite the fact that since he had left Vendée he had not been to Mass, and religion had never much concerned him. Had these words, perhaps, an incantatory value for him?

He was in *limbo*. He was part of the household without having his place in it, was the master but without a master's rights, and he loved without being sure of loving.

Admittedly, he no longer needed to deceive as he had had to before, but it came to the same thing in the long run.

Perhaps another word was more accurate? Hadn't Berthe, at the time that she had settled his future, *excommunicated* him?

He caught himself suspecting people of thoughts which almost certainly they did not have. When Pascali came to drink his glass of wine, he now used to wonder what went on inside his head, that head like an apostle's in a stained-glass window, or a bandit's, for the mason might well have been one as much as the other.

Why, one fine morning, had Pascali brought his daughter, still only a child, to La Bastide? It was to Émile, not to Berthe, that he had entrusted her. And Pascali must know men.

Since then, every time he came and sat in the kitchen, wasn't it to see how Émile and Ada were getting on?

Hadn't he guessed, and hadn't what had happened been what he wanted? In this way Ada would not hang about in the streets of Mouans-Sartoux and the dance halls, passing from the arms of one boy to those of another, only to return home one day pregnant.

All this was probably false, but for weeks now he had thought like someone in a fever, enlarging some things in his mind, creating others out of nothing. At certain moments he became so unsure of himself as to wonder whether it were not he who was in the wrong and Berthe who was right.

It was impossible for things to last like this. It is claimed that a man can live a long time without eating or drinking. It is more difficult to live without one's pride, and his wife had taken his away.

He would never forgive her.

How long did this phase, the most painful of all, last? The same time, more or less, as a real illness, three or four weeks. He had no more points of reference, because he no longer noticed the days.

And it was in an unexpected fashion that he emerged from it. It happened on the hottest Sunday of the year, with cars crowding on all the roads, the beaches covered with bathers, people storming into the restaurants at Cannes, where they simply could not cater to everybody.

There were customers in shorts, women in bathing costumes, children crying, and Jean-Claude never stopped uncorking bottles of *rosé*. Some would be asking for the bowls so as to be able to play beneath the terrace, others wanted sandwiches, to go and eat in the mountains.

As on every other Sunday he had put *bouillabaisse* and calamary risotto on the menu, but he hadn't been able to get all the fish he would have liked from the fishermen. He had a leg of mutton in the oven, cold meat in the refrigerator.

From half-past twelve the terrace had begun to fill up and, at the moment when Berthe was about to sit down in her usual corner, two large American cars had drawn up, disgorging a dozen people between the two of them.

"Can we eat?"

Jean-Claude had come in to announce:

"Twelve more lunches."

Juice from the mutton was draining onto the wood of the table, the saucepans were steaming, the air smelled of fish, garlic, boiling oil.

"Warn them there won't be enough *bouillabaisse* or risotto for everybody."

Berthe was serving *apéritifs* to the new arrivals. They were all talking, laughing, moving about, and Maubi was constantly having to go down to the cellar.

"Madame is asking what she can have to eat."

He ought to have put aside a helping of risotto, as it was her favorite dish, which she ate every Sunday, but he hadn't done so. The mutton was nearly ready. He was already carving the cold meat he had reserved for dinner.

"Ask her if she would like me to open a tin of something."

The staff would eat from it as well. It was not the first time.

"What did she say?"

"She would like some *cassoulet*."

In the way of tinned food, apart from sardines, tunny fish, different kinds of fruit in syrup, they had chiefly *cassoulet* and concoctions with sauerkraut. It was not the season for eating these things, but they had no choice.

He opened the cupboard, selected one of the large two-quart tins sold specially to restaurants. The label was pockmarked with rust, he noticed, without attaching any importance to it, since that often happened.

It was past three o'clock when the terrace finally cleared and the activity died down. Émile, who had hastily swallowed an anchovy here, an olive or crust of bread there, was no longer hungry and, taking off his cap and apron, he emptied a glass of wine before heading for the Cabin.

He had made no sign to Ada. In all the confusion he had hardly noticed her. In the kitchen the staff were beginning to eat, before setting about the massive washing up.

This time he slept, exhausted. He had not locked the door. It took him a good while to come to his senses when somebody shook his shoulder, and he did not understand what was happening to him when he saw Jean-Claude, in his white jacket, bending over him.

"Monsieur Émile! . . . Monsieur Émile! . . . Come quickly! . . ."

"What's the matter?"

"Madame . . ."

At first he thought it was an accident, perhaps a dispute with some customers, a brawl.

"She is very ill. She says she is going to die."

"Did she send for me?"

"I don't know. I didn't go up."

He crossed through a patch of sun, found the shade again on entering the house. Ada was standing at the foot of the stairs. Their eyes met, and it seemed to him the girl's expression was more intense than usual.

"Who is up there with her?"

"Madame Lavaud and Madame Maubi."

He went up, and at that moment he would have been unable to say what he was hoping. He saw Berthe, bending over a basin beside the bed, her face crimson, trying in vain to vomit.

"You must . . ." Madame Lavaud was saying. "Make another effort. . . . Stick your finger in your mouth. . . ."

Berthe's eyelids were swollen with tears. Noticing Émile, she stammered:

"I'm going to die. . . ."

"Has somebody telephoned the doctor?"

"You realize Dr. Guérini's out in his boat," replied Madame Maubi. "It's Sunday."

"And Chouard?"

"I think my husband has phoned him."

He went downstairs, not sure where he ought to be.

"It must be the *cassoulet* and the heat," Maubi was explaining. "I once saw a whole wedding ill on account of the *foie gras*, and two of them even died."

"Was Chouard at home?"

"He was asleep."

It was not long before he arrived, pushing his bicycle up the hill, for he no longer dared to drive a car.

"What has she had to eat?"

"We had an overflow of customers. I opened a tin of *cassoulet*."

"Did anybody else have it as well?"

He wasn't sure. He turned to Maubi, who nodded affirmatively.

87

"The entire kitchen."

"Nobody else ill?"

Chouard went up. Émile didn't follow him, sat down in the nearest chair and mopped himself.

"We suddenly heard groans," Maubi was saying. "Then a voice calling for help. . . ."

Once again, Émile's eyes met Ada's.

Was everything resolving itself, just at the moment they least expected it?

He felt no pity for Berthe. He had had none for Big Louis either, when he had died. At Champagné, as a child, he had grown used to people and animals dying, and sometimes his father would kill a calf or a pig in the yard; he himself had learned as a small child to cut the throats of chickens and ducks.

It was more a sort of peace which descended upon him, a sudden relaxation.

His fever was abating. He looked around him with his eyes clear once more, and told himself:

"I mustn't seem to be indifferent or, worse still, relieved."

To occupy himself, he went into the kitchen.

"What's happened to the empty tin?"

"It's in the garbage pail."

He went and searched for it himself, rummaging without revulsion among the leftovers from the meal, and the guts of the fishes. A short while later, he placed the tin on the table, after sniffing it.

"It doesn't smell."

There were the traces of rust, but because of the climate most of the tins in the cupboard bore similar marks.

Ada, too, seemed more at ease, but wasn't it from seeing him relaxed at last?

He went and poured himself a glass of spirits, gave one to Madame Lavaud, who had just come downstairs and was clasping her bosom as if she was going to be ill as well.

"Drink that."

"Oh, it's not the *cassoulet* I'm afraid of. My stomach will digest anything. It's just seeing her like that . . ."

"What is the doctor doing?"

"He has called for hot water, lots of hot water. I fetched some from the bathroom, and now . . ."

The few customers still left on the terrace were asking what had happened. Jean-Claude didn't know what to say to them.

"Tell them Madame has been taken ill."

Impatience overcame him, and he ended by going upstairs and listening at the door. He heard nothing but hiccoughs, water being poured into the basin, a little at a time, Chouard's voice repeating monotonously:

"Relax. . . . Don't tense yourself. . . . There's nothing to be afraid of. . . ."

He himself cannot have been at his best at this time of day. Dragged from his siesta, he was almost certainly suffering from a hangover, and Émile went and fetched him a glass of brandy, half opened the door.

"For you, Doctor."

They had removed Berthe's clothes, and she had only a Turkish towel around her stomach. Seated in a chair, bent double, with her mouth open, she was staring at the basin placed at her feet, but she had time to raise her eyes toward her husband.

He preferred to shut the door again, a shade paler. He didn't know where to go and, after a quarter of an hour spent wandering from the dining room on to the terrace and into the kitchen, he decided to start on the dinner.

When he finally heard Chouard's footsteps on the stairs, he went to meet him, with his cap on his head, automatically collected the bottle of cognac on the way.

"How is she?"

"I've given her an injection and she is beginning to sleep. I thought for a moment of sending her to the hospital or to a clinic, but I had a child to get to hospital urgently this morning and I couldn't find a bed free in Cannes or even in Nice. There have been so many car accidents, congestions caused by the sun or bathing in the sea. . . ."

Chouard asked in his turn:

"What about the others?"

"The staff hasn't complained of anything."

To save himself the trouble of shaving, Chouard wore a full reddish beard, and he had immense bushy eyebrows.

"Her father," he grunted, after emptying his glass, "was almost as much of a drunkard as I am, and probably her grandfather was as well. She has inherited a bad liver, which doesn't dispose of toxic elements as it should, and I wouldn't be surprised if some day or other she doesn't have to have her gall bladder removed."

Émile didn't know what Ada was doing in the room, but she was there.

For the space of a second their eyes met once again.

"Will she pull through?" he asked.

"Today, yes. But next time, I'm not so sure."

Chouard shrugged his shoulders.

"It's the same old story. She ought to keep to a strict diet, and she won't. One fine day, when she eats a dish which doesn't agree with her . . ."

The house was so peaceful, after the excitement of the rest of the day, that it almost seemed like being in church.

Ada was still there, waiting for God knows what, and, as if he were making a sudden decision, Émile looked at her insistently as though to transmit a message, then blinked his eyelids two or three times.

This had happened eleven months ago and he hadn't once been tempted to turn back. As a result of this fortuitous incident, he had arrived unexpectedly at a conclusion and he could see no other way out.

Straight away, he had regained a certain interior peace. He had still slept, that night, and on the following ones, beside Berthe. When she had waked up, toward three o'clock in the morning, he had helped her to the bathroom and had waited to bring her back to bed.

Next morning, she had said to him in a still lugubrious voice:

"Thank you for looking after me."

That could no longer touch him. He had rounded a certain point, and hardly even noticed it, and everything that had happened before had lost its importance.

He no longer asked himself any questions. To be more exact, the questions which he asked himself now were precise ones, powerless to trouble him, technical questions in a way.

For example, he had discovered that it would have to take place on a Sunday, so that Dr. Guérini would be out at sea and Chouard would be called in.

The season was already too far advanced. Soon, the tourists would return home, and the calm of autumn, then of winter, would make the thing more difficult, too obvious.

That Sunday, Berthe could have died without most of the customers realizing it, and the burial, three days later, would not have caused any stir.

"What I don't understand is why I should have been the only person to be ill."

"Chouard told us: because of your liver."

She stayed in bed all day on Monday, but in the evening she came downstairs to make out the bills of the guests who were leaving.

He had said nothing to anybody, not even to Ada. Between her and him, there had been nothing but a look, and Berthe was not then present.

Yet he would have sworn that, from that moment, Berthe had her suspicions. Granted, she had always kept watch on her husband, but she was doing so now as if a fixed idea was obsessing her.

Did she imagine he had tried to poison her? He knew that she asked questions in the kitchen, and she had had the tin of *cassoulet* shown to her.

This did not bother Émile, for she would have time to forget it, to reassure herself. And, when he had accomplished what he had decided to accomplish, he certainly hoped she would be past talking about it.

Already before the incident of the *cassoulet*, he had thought of an almost analogous solution, but the solution was a bad one and he had rejected it without further ado.

His idea, in fact, had been to take Berthe out to sea with him. She couldn't swim. He would choose a day with the *mistral* blowing and would steer her out beyond the islands. On his return, he would simply have to say that she had been leaning over the side and had lost her footing.

It was no good. He was a good swimmer and people would ask why he had not fished her out. Besides, he would have had difficulty in persuading his wife, suspicious as she was, to accompany him in the boat.

At the very least, he would have had to get her into the habit of going out fishing with him, take her often, to start with in calm weather, then, little by little, on rougher seas.

That idea had been dropped a long time ago. It had not even been a plan, merely a sort of daydream.

Like the one—but it was still more absurd—of cleaning his revolver in front of her, or his sporting rifle. One often reads, in the newspapers, accounts of accidents of this kind. Émile would pretend he didn't know the gun was loaded.

He gave the matter no further thought, and he had almost resigned himself to his situation once and for all, when Chouard had unwittingly provided him with the solution.

At present, the perfecting of his plan kept him sufficiently busy for him no longer to think about anything else, and for his life to become almost enjoyable. When Ada came to him in the Cabin, he did not speak about anything to her, but when he took her in his arms he was relaxed, smiling. He said only: "I'm happy."

A good month elapsed before he murmured in her ear:

"One day, we shall be in the big bed together, as when 'she' was in Luçon."

He wanted to leave nothing to chance, and that was why he avoided going to a library in Cannes or Nice. Nor again would he buy the books he needed, as that would be dangerous.

To go to Marseilles, where he wasn't known, he had to wait until the end of the season and, until then, he tried not to make his plan too detailed, for everything he might elaborate now might not hold good later on.

It was another phase. These phases were following one another, each more or less different from the last.

This one was peaceful, rather hazy, with a certain unreality.

He went through the motions of the daily routine, began playing bowls again, went to the market. Soon he would put his boat to sea again after having given it a coat of underwater paint.

There still remained, between the real world and himself, a slight disconnection.

"Next summer . . ."

He derived a subtle satisfaction from being the only person, or almost the only person—for there was Ada—to know.

People might suppose that he was nothing more than a sort of servant of Berthe's, and some of them probably thought he had married her for her money, for La Bastide.

It could no longer humiliate him. He felt like telling them:

"Just you wait!"

He would prove to them that he was not a May bug on the end of a line, a canary in its cage, a sorry fellow the mother and daughter had bought to run their restaurant.

People would obviously never know, and he began to regret it. He must be careful, afterwards, not to be too tempted to boast.

Berthe was watching him more than ever, and he was glad since, had it been necessary, this would have removed his last hesitations.

He waited until November, when his mother-in-law was there, to mention the trip to Marseilles. For some time they had been having trouble with the water pump, as the water works did not serve La Bastide and they had to pump their supply by means of a motor.

An expert from Cannes had come, had done some repairs, and a week later they had had another breakdown.

Émile had cut a Marseilles firm's advertisement out of the newspaper.

"As soon as I have a moment I'll go and see for myself."

It was to prevent Berthe from coming with him that he had awaited the arrival of his mother-in-law. He had not given the two women time to arrange and plan a trip to Marseilles for themselves as well.

One morning he had come downstairs, dressed for town.

"Where are you going?"

"Marseilles. I told you about it a month ago."

He had purposely made just a vague allusion to the trip a month before.

"It's our only chance of installing a new pump. . . ."

She was suspicious, looked at him to read into his thoughts. He didn't care, for she could read nothing. It was too late. It was as though he had already pressed the button to set the machine in motion.

"When will you be back?"

"Tonight or tomorrow. It depends on what I find there."

As he passed in front of Ada, he had been unable to prevent himself from murmuring:

"Only a few months more!"

It was up to her to understand or not to understand. It made no difference to him. Nothing made any difference to him. He was taking action. He was past turning back, tormenting himself, wondering whether his decision was just or unjust.

From now on he was following a precise plan, and he was humming to himself as he left Saint-Charles Station, knowing in advance which way to go.

He remembered that in public libraries, municipal or otherwise, readers fill in forms, and he did not want to leave telltale documents behind him. Besides, these libraries would not necessarily have the volumes he needed.

He had found in the telephone book, well before his journey, an address which sounded right to him: "Blanchot, University Bookshop."

Now there was a School of Medicine at Marseilles. Émile still looked young enough to pass as a student. The shop was vast, with shelves piled with books to the ceiling, and, luckily, the different sections were indicated by placards.

Having located the bookshop, he saw to the pump, as he preferred to get down to work in the middle of the afternoon, when there would be enough people for him to pass unnoticed.

Others, like himself, were leafing through books, some of them perched on ladders, and it took him only a few moments to put his hand on a volume which interested him: *Poison, Its Nature and Effects*, by Charles Leleux.

It was not the work of a doctor, but of a lawyer of the Paris Court of Appeal, and part of the volume was devoted to the most celebrated cases of arsenic poisoning.

Without reading it all, by glancing through certain chapters, he already got the reassuring impression that in most cases the poisoning had only been discovered by accident, usually as a result of clumsiness.

More technical details were provided by another book he found on the same shelf:

Modern Toxicology, by Professor Roger Douris.

"CHAPTER VIII—*Arsenic and Its Compounds*."

On the next page:

"CRIMINAL POISONING."

". . . *Criminals chiefly have recourse to arsenious anhydride, a white floury powder. Arsenious anhydride, which does not easily dissolve in liquids, is liable to persist on the surface of food and be noticed by the victim. . . .*"

". . . *Criminal poisoning by means of arsenic is very frequent and has been known since earliest times. . . .*"

The word *criminal* did not shock him. By no means. He watched the comings and goings around him. A young shop-girl asked him, without bothering about what he was reading:

"Have you found what you are looking for?"

"Not yet."

". . . *Use of arsenious acid for destroying vermin, foxes, rats, weasels . . .*"

"*Compounds of arsenic are also used in agriculture to counteract plagues of certain kinds of insect. . . .*"

". . . *Arsenate of lead gives excellent results. Many tons of this salt are used each year by agricultural workers. . . .*"

He stopped at a more detailed passage:

"*Toxic doses.—In general, consumption of 0.20 grammes of arsenious acid will result in a peracute intoxication leading to death in a few hours (10 to 24).*"

Twenty-four hours was too long, as Dr. Guérini would have time to come in from fishing and it might occur to somebody, perhaps Chouard himself, to call him in for consultation.

There was a list of other poisons, with their effects, the ways of detecting them, the antidotes to apply, but nearly all of them appeared to be difficult to get hold of.

He opened a third volume, thicker than the previous ones:

Summary of Toxic Chemistry, by F. Schoofs, Professor Emeritus of the Faculty of Medicine in the University of Liége.

He immediately looked through the list of contents. He did not want to attract attention by remaining too long in the bookshop; if necessary, he would return in two or three weeks.

"CAUSES OF POISONING

"*Since arsenic is a very well-known toxic and easily accessible to the public, it will be understood that it is a frequent cause of accidental and criminal poisoning, or of suicides.*

"*In one case of criminal poisoning, a powdered arseniferous ore was mixed with pepper. . . .*"

Further on:

". . . *According to the dose and method of administration arsenical intoxication can take on an acute or a chronic form; whatever the form, the same symptoms appear and in the same order; gastrointestinal disturbances, laryngeal catarrh and bronchitis, cutaneous eruptions, paralysis of the lower limbs. . . .*"

Gastroenteritis, Berthe had just had. Not only had Chouard not been surprised, but he was prepared for further recurrences. Every year, besides, she had had two or three sore throats, since her throat was easily infected.

He would have liked to take notes. It wasn't wise. He preferred to learn certain passages by heart, as at school, and that done, he picked out a book on childbirth which he went and showed to the girl at the counter.

"How much is this?"

She looked for the price inscribed in pencil inside the cover and he paid, spent a good quarter of an hour wandering among side-streets before disposing of the book.

That morning he had made no definite decision about the pump and the motor, so as to leave open for himself, if necessary, the possibility of another trip. As it was no longer necessary, he went into the shop to confirm his order.

It was a fine day and he strolled along the Canebière, took an *apéritif* on a café terrace, and gazed at the passers-by.

Maubi used a product with an arsenic base for the cherry orchard, which he sprayed twice a year on the trees, but there was nothing to indicate that this product contained enough poison.

In the tool shed, a box marked with a skull and crossbones contained a grayish paste which had been used only a short time ago for killing rats and moles. Maubi spread it like butter on scraps of bread or cheese, and afterwards one would find the animals shriveled up.

Émile had vaguely read the directions, before knowing that he would one day need some poison. He had no idea whether the box was half full or nearly empty. Everything in its own good time. He would see to it at the proper moment.

For the present, he was satisfied with what he had learned. Nobody had taken any notice of him. He was almost certain that the assistant at the bookshop would not recognize him in the street. She did not know his name, nor where he came from. And finally he had taken care to buy a book on an entirely different subject.

He reached La Bastide at ten o'clock in the evening, found the two women, mother and daughter, in the dining room, where they had left only one light on.

Had Berthe spoken to her mother about what had happened between them? It was hardly likely. Her pride must have held her back, even with the old woman.

He announced, helping himself to a glass of wine:

"I've bought a motor pump. They are coming to install it in ten days' time."

He put a catalogue on the table and walked toward the stairs. "Good night."

He was not running away from her, but considered himself as not belonging to the family. He did not wait for his wife to come to bed. They no longer said good morning or good night to one another. And finally he avoided as far as possible letting her see him naked, or even half naked.

Berthe did not have the same feeling of modesty and undressed as she had done in the past, which embarrassed him and made him turn away. He could scarcely remember the intimacy their bodies had known. It had left no trace, and his wife's flesh was more alien to him than that of any of the women guests.

What surprised him was that he had been capable, at one period, of placing his lips to those of Berthe.

He was still accepting, for a certain time, her presence in the house, in his bed; he accepted speaking to her when there was no way around it, but he practically regarded their cohabitation as a monstrous obligation.

What was she busy telling her mother about, before coming upstairs to undress in the dark?

But what was the point of thinking about it, since in a few months it would all be over?

SEVEN

He sometimes asked himself, with what seemed to him justifiable pride, whether anybody had ever planned a crime with so much lucidity and meticulousness as he was doing now. At the outset, he used to avoid that word, then, one fine day, he had realized that this was almost to walk with bowed head, to be ashamed, and he had taken to calling things by their correct names.

It was a pity, really, that there was nobody to observe him during these months of preparation, to follow the train of his thought, to appreciate the intricate mechanism which an enterprise of this kind brought into play, for he had more and more the conviction that he was undergoing an exceptional experience.

Unfortunately, there was only himself to watch himself living. And if there were two women to observe him, they did so from two very different standpoints.

Since the exchange of glances at the time of Berthe's illness, he had been convinced that Ada knew, that she had had the same idea as he, at the same moment. But with her it had been simply the sudden discovery of a chance, of a way out, and probably she would never have developed it to the point of action.

Ever since she had seen him passing, gradually, to the phase of bringing things about, she had become less sure of herself, and sometimes, during the siesta, she would lie inert in his arms, her thoughts elsewhere.

Misunderstanding her, he would whisper:

"It won't be long now, Ada!"

The time he saw a shiver run through her from her head to her feet, he understood. Besides, she had the frankness to admit:

"I'm afraid."

"What of?"

"I don't know."

"You mustn't be afraid. There's nothing to be frightened of. Do you know what 'legitimate defense' means?"

She nodded her head.

"Well! My case is one of legitimate defense. It's me or her. Would you rather it was me?"

She answered no, of course not. Indeed it wasn't so much to reassure her, nor to whitewash himself, nor again to banish her scruples, that he spoke in this way. He believed it. It was in fact Berthe or himself. Perhaps not entirely in this sense, but it came to the same thing.

It wasn't he who had started it. He had never tried to oppress anyone. The proof was that everybody in the country had adopted him and liked him, while Berthe remained not only an outsider but an enemy.

He was defending what was most precious to him, no matter whether it was called vanity, self-esteem, or pride, and as far as he was concerned he knew that he was not proud, that he asked simply to be allowed to live the life of a man.

Berthe went on watching him, not to say spying on him, as she had always done. Though it had exasperated Émile so much in the past, before his decision, now it acted as a kind of spur.

Not only did she thus render the outcome still more inevitable, but the game became more difficult and therefore more exciting.

He sensed that she was intrigued by his change of mood, and every time he began humming, not to irritate her, but because he really was in a good humor, she could not prevent herself from giving a start, then looking at him to try to understand.

She was acquiring the habit of coming into the kitchen a dozen times a day, though she had no business there, and she occasionally opened the store cupboard, the refrigerator, lifted the lids off the saucepans.

Was she thinking of poison? It was quite likely. And the moment came when he went a step further, when he wondered whether she wasn't planning independently to poison him. Isn't poisoning, in most cases, a woman's crime? This, too, he had learned in Marseilles.

As he was in charge of the kitchen and he seldom took a regular meal, it was more difficult for her to do than it was for him.

As for guessing the reasons behind his actions and behavior, cunning though she was, Berthe would never be able to do it.

Chance—doesn't chance always back the one who is in the right?—had brought him to the discovery of another treatise, a book he had not seen on the shelves of the Marseilles bookshop and which dealt in more precise terms than the others.

One morning, as he was cleaning the fish, a hogfish spike had caught under his thumbnail, and he had tried in vain to extract it with the point of a penknife, then with a pair of pincers. Madame Lavaud had tried too. Now everybody on the Riviera knows that cuts caused by hogfish have a tendency to turn septic.

In the afternoon, instead of taking a siesta, he had decided to go and see Dr. Chouard, who would have the necessary instruments. So he had gone to Pégomas, where he had been surprised to find the house, which was usually so dilapidated, looking almost clean. He had rung the bell. A girl of about thirty, well formed and attractive, whom he didn't know, had opened the door.

"Is the doctor in?"

"You're the owner of La Bastide, aren't you?"

He wondered how she had recognized him, and was pleased.

"Come in. The doctor has gone to take a patient to hospital, but he won't be long."

So Chouard had replaced old Paola, who had probably become useless, with this pretty girl who had managed to clean the house from top to bottom. Was she his mistress? It was possible, probable even.

And that pleased him, ultimately, for it proved . . .

No matter what it proved. He understood himself. He was not like Chouard, was not the same age and, moreover, he was not a drunkard. All the same there were points in common, or to be more accurate there might be one day.

"Come in, Monsieur Émile."

She knew his first name as well. She did not leave him in the almost gloomy waiting room, but opened the padded door of the consulting room.

"I'll ring the hospital and tell him you're here."

She dialed the number. She was very different from Ada, who never seemed to have washed. Her bosom was ample, her hips and thighs well covered, and she smelled of cleanliness and soap, while her rather full lips parted naturally in a smile.

"Broussailles Hospital? Is Dr. Chouard still there? . . . Yes. . . . I'll wait. . . ."

She explained to Émile:

"When he left he told me he was just going in and coming back in the bus."

And, into the receiver:

"Hello. . . . Is that you, sir? . . . It's Germaine here. . . . I wanted to know if you were coming back, because Monsieur Émile is here in your consulting room. . . . From La Bastide, yes. . . . What? . . ."

She turned to Émile.

"Is it for yourself?"

He nodded.

"It's for himself. . . . No, he isn't in a hurry. . . . All right! I'll tell him. . . ."

Then, hanging up:

"He is catching the bus in five minutes. I must go upstairs to finish doing the bedroom. You will find some magazines . . ."

The shutters were three-quarters closed, as in most houses on the Riviera, and the shade was cool. The shelves on the wall overflowed with books, and he ran his eyes mechanically over their titles.

It was in this way that he came across a large volume, bound in gray cloth, with a blue title-label reading: *Legal and Judiciary Medicine.*

Curious to see whether it mentioned arsenic poisoning, he soon found some sections far more explicit than the ones in Marseilles. Here there was nobody to watch him. Chouard would be a good half-hour reaching Pégomas in the bus, and this gave Émile time to commit to memory what he needed to know.

". . . *The peracute form (arsenical cholera) produces the symptoms of a choleraic type of gastroenteritis: painful vomiting, at first alimentary, then consisting of bile and blood, is followed by colic; abundant serous diarrhea, in rice-water particles; violent thirst; constriction of the throat; anuresis; cramps; petechiae; sensation of cold in the limbs; hypothermia; quickening, weakness, and irregularity of the pulse, ending in collapse in a few hours, 24 at the maximum . . ."*

He was amazed to find that he understood almost everything. "Rice-water" no doubt had something to do with rice. "Hypothermia" meant a general lowering of the temperature. Practically only "anuresis" and "petechiae" remained wrapped in mystery.

This information confirmed that the symptoms resembled, only in more serious form, those which Berthe had shown after eating the tinned *cassoulet.*

And wasn't it Chouard himself who had spoken of her bad liver and gall bladder?

"Acute form.—The symptoms develop an hour or two after ingestion of the poison, with gastrointestinal disorders, accompanied by a burning sensation, violent thirst and ptyalism. . . ."

He didn't understand the word "ptyalism" either, but the rest still held good.

He glanced through the pages, pausing now and then at a paragraph, his lips moving as when he learned his lessons as a schoolboy.

"The difficulty of making a precise diagnosis explains the frequency of successive acts of poisoning by the same individual, who can trust that he will not be brought to account until the day when the recurrence and similarity of the episodes provide a clue for the diagnosis."

That was the most interesting sentence of all. Didn't it prove that by poisoning only one person, in favorable conditions—which was the case with Berthe, who had already shown almost identical symptoms—and by taking all possible precautions, he was running no risk?

He made sure he put the book back exactly in its place, and he opened a magazine long before Chouard's return. If his new servant had put some order into the house, the doctor himself remained the same, with a faint smell of wine still hanging around the thick, reddish hair of his beard.

His hand trembled a little, with the trembling of alcoholics, as he pulled the spike from Émile's thumb.

"How are things up there? It's a good while since I called."

He gave a wink, with a jerk of his head toward the door, to explain that it was on account of Germaine. He was lascivious by nature, and there were stories of scandals with women patients he had made undress without any reason. There had even been talk of bringing him before the Medical Council.

At the stage he had reached, it made no difference to him; nothing made any difference to him; he laughed at everything, like a faun or a satyr, and he probably had no more faith in medicine than in humanity.

"How is our charming Berthe?"

The irony underlining the word "charming" delighted Émile.

"Still a bit seedy. Every so often she complains of pains, sometimes her stomach and sometimes her throat."

This gave him an idea, which he forthwith put into practice. When he went to play bowls at Mouans-Sartoux, people asked after his wife, even people who knew her only by sight. They had even given her a nickname, which a few of them risked using to his face.

"How's the frigidaire?"

Instead of replying carelessly that she was all right, he now found a short phrase which he would let fall lightly.

"The same old liver trouble. . . ."

Or else:

"She still has her colic. . . ."

And, to ring the changes:

"If she did what the doctor told her, she wouldn't eat anything except spaghetti and boiled vegetables."

It all fell like drops of water. Which advertisement is it that says every drop counts? It would all come back to people's memories one day and would help them to regard the outcome as natural.

He was lost in the technique of the thing, and anybody would have thought he was refining it for the pleasure of doing so. He was convinced, in his own mind, that none of the precautions he was taking was superfluous.

He had read, like everybody else, accounts of poisoners' trials in the newspapers. Nine times out of ten, if they were finally convicted, it was by discovery of the way the poison had been obtained.

At La Bastide there were vines, fruit trees, fields in which it was normal to destroy meadow mice, and only recently Madame Lavaud had reported the presence of rats in the cellar.

He could have gone to the chemist in Mouans-Sartoux, or Les Baraques, or any chemist in Cannes to buy arsenic, and nobody would be surprised at the time.

That was what nearly all the others had done before him and what, in the long run, had been their undoing.

There was a product with an arsenic base in the tool shed. In the normal course of events Émile virtually never set foot there. There was nothing, apparently, to stop him going in there under some pretext or other, and even without pretext, since the shed was part of the estate.

He preferred to take his time. And he took advantage of an incident of two years ago, for one must know how to take advantage of everything. One Sunday when he had been busy and there was no basil left in the house, he had rounded on Maubi.

"I've been asking for a plot to be kept for herbs in the kitchen garden for months now. I spend my time buying them in the market, as though we didn't even have a patch of land. . . ."

Since then Maubi had contented himself with planting some thyme, which had soon died, near the low wall.

Émile chose a morning when Berthe was busy with her accounts in the dining room, where she always sat at the same table near the window. The kitchen door was open, as usual.

"Have you seen to my kitchen herbs yet?" he asked Maubi in a loud voice.

"Not yet, but . . ."

"Don't bother. I'll do it myself. . . ."

He was known to be handy at most things. He was also known

to be happy to work out of doors, and one year it was he who had copper-sulphated the vines.

"I'll prepare the ground and tomorrow I'll go and see the nurseryman. . . ."

It was entertaining. Berthe was listening. Did she wonder what he was up to? However sharp she might be, he defied her to divine his exact intentions.

He did in fact go and prepare some ground, which meant he could enter the shed to fetch the necessary tools.

He made no pretense. He worked with care. Finding two frames which had not been used for a long time and were missing several panes, he decided to prepare a forcing bed as well.

Thus all winter he would have chives, parsley, chervil, sorrel, and purslane.

The tin box was half full of arsenical paste, and he removed a little more than a cubic half-inch, which he wrapped in greaseproof paper and stuffed into his pocket.

In the kitchen he would have to be careful, not only on account of Madame Lavaud, who was nearly always there, but because of Berthe, who, walking soundlessly, would come in and prowl about with a falsely innocent air.

But he found an opportunity to make a meat ball and insert the grayish paste, and took it off with him one afternoon. He was generally supposed to have gone to Mouans-Sartoux to buy some panes of glass and putty to repair the frame.

In fact, wanting to leave nothing to chance, he had resolved to make an experiment. The treatises on poison spoke of 0.20 grammes as a fatal dose, but this referred not to a compound but to the pure product, which was not what he had.

A little short of Mouans-Sartoux, not far from Pascali's house, there was a shack on the side of the road by a turning, inhabited by an old man who worked at the quarry. He was a widower, who lived alone with his dog, a large yellowish animal, scarcely able to walk and half blind.

A hundred times Émile had seen it on the roadside, sprawled in the shade, with red circles around its eyes, dragging itself reluctantly to its feet to retreat a few paces as the sun advanced.

Opposite, the hedge was thick. On the side of the house there was nothing to prevent people from seeing if there was anybody in the vineyard.

He made sure as he passed that there was nobody about and, without slowing down, threw out the meat ball, which landed almost at the dog's feet.

He bought his glass panes and his putty, made use of the opportunity to play a game of *pétanque* with the landlord of the Golden Crown. The postman and the cobbler watched the game. The weather was fine, fairly cool, and he drank two glasses of white wine before going back up the hill to La Bastide.

He had seen the dog again as he passed. The meat ball had disappeared.

Next day the dog was in its usual place. The following day as well. He tried the experiment again and got the same results.

The proportion of arsenic in the compound was evidently too slight. Though he knew how to remedy this, it introduced new complications, new methods of approach, and this was why, two days later, he began lighting a fire, in the afternoon, in the hearth in the Cabin.

Although he seldom did so, there was nothing extraordinary about it. The building was cool and damp, and the windows were rarely opened; it was only by accident that the shutters were unlatched.

It was quite natural for him to remove the mustiness from the air, for his siesta, by burning a few vine-stocks.

"I think I'm going to light myself a fire. . . ."

It was still in the kitchen that he said this, and still at a time when he knew Berthe to be in the next room.

"Considering the time the chimney was last swept, you'll be smoked out."

He thought for a moment it was true. The smoke came back into the room, but he used a pair of bellows and when the flames were high enough the chimney suddenly drew with a sucking sound.

He couldn't use one of the kitchen saucepans. Nor did he dare to buy a small aluminum pan from a store.

This experiment alone took more than a fortnight all told. He found an old tin can which had been opened fairly neatly, used it as a container, and instead of going to sleep—having taken care, of course, not to give the signal to Ada—he devoted himself to his spot of cooking.

First of all he added the arsenic paste to a certain quantity of water. Then he boiled the whole mixture, not too fast, over a low fire, until there was only a little whitish matter left in the bottom of the tin.

He scooped it out with a piece of wood, mixed it with some minced meat, and once again the meat ball was thrown to the dog.

In the meantime he had sown some seeds beneath the two frames and ordered some seedlings. Everything fitted in. His comings and goings were logical. He was not risking a single suspicious move.

The dose was still not strong enough. He almost allowed himself to become discouraged when he found the dog in its place next day, and he nourished a veritable hatred for this old beast which refused to die.

He started again, not immediately, but three days later, and he had taken care to go out fishing as he usually did at this time of year.

Finally, by boiling down his mixture several times, he obtained a powder with metallic glints in it, and on the next day, not seeing the dog, he realized that he had succeeded.

Nor did he see the animal again on the following days.

He played a lot of bowls, nearly every afternoon, for this was the way to discover whether there had been any rumors.

If the owner of the dog had suspected that his animal had been poisoned, he would not have failed to speak about it and the talk would have reached the village. Somebody would certainly have turned up, in that case, and said:

"By the way, old Manuel's dog has been poisoned."

Nothing. Not a word. Only a patch of freshly dug earth in the small garden, opposite the house.

That meant the animal's death had seemed natural.

There remained one experiment to try, the most disagreeable one, and it was necessary to wait for a Sunday. The books he had read spoke of the taste and smell which in many cases had aroused the suspicions of the intended victims.

In one case, in Scotland, the arsenic had been put into some very hot chocolate and the victim had suspected nothing. But Berthe did not drink chocolate and she never drank anything very hot. The book stressed the fact that the chocolate had been *boiling*.

It mentioned a smell similar to that of garlic, which would be found afterwards in the vomit and evacuations.

Now there existed one dish on which Berthe doted, indeed the principal specialty of La Bastide, which all the regular customers asked for and which appeared on the menu once a week, on Sundays: it was the calamary risotto.

He little suspected, at the time when he had been perfecting the recipe—for he had improved on the recipe he had been given —he little suspected that it would one day be invaluable to him. He was lucky in that, as he had been over the herbs, and in his habit of taking a siesta in the Cabin. Everything had its use in the end. One would have thought that providence . . .

He had to allow three Sundays to pass, for it was not so easy as it might seem to remove a portion of risotto without being spotted.

Using the experience he had acquired with the dog, he measured out a certain quantity of powder, which he mixed with the rice soaked in the sauce. At first, a few bright specks remained. Then, little by little, they became absorbed in the ink of the squid, which provided the base for the sauce.

Émile wanted to be sure that the dish had no smell, or anything suspicious about its appearance. Last of all, it was essential to taste it.

He took only a small mouthful, of course, had the courage not to spit it out again. The rice had no suspicious taste. It remained to be seen whether he would feel sick, and he stretched out in the shade, attentive to the reactions of his stomach.

Did his imagination play some part in it? There was no way of telling for sure. The fact remains that he was seized with fits of nausea. He forced himself not to vomit, and toward five o'clock he resumed his normal work, not without feeling drops of sweat on his brow.

Two or three times, as he passed, he looked at himself in the glass, and there was no doubt that he was pale.

It was February. He had spent almost the entire winter at it, preparing enough powder so that, if it should fail the first time, he should be able to start again.

Now that he had finished with the material items, he occupied his mind with putting the finishing touches to the other details, fixing a date for example, then rehearsing all that he would have to do.

One incident disturbed him for a while, since, by its consequences, it might have altered a great many other things. Not only did Madame Maubi come to help in the kitchen and with the housework during the season but, during the rest of the year, on Madame Lavaud's day off, it was she who took her place.

She was a fairly large woman, with feet that caused her pain, and when she arrived she changed from her shoes into felt slippers. In summer, she would take off her dress and put on an overall with a small black-and-white checked pattern. She carried both slippers and overall in a straw bag of the kind used by housewives in the Midi for doing their market shopping.

Émile had never paid any attention to these details, which were part of the household routine. Two or three times he had had occasion to remark:

"Strange! There are only three tins of sardines left. . . ."

Or:

"I thought I had left some sausage in the refrigerator. . . ."

One evening, when he was at the bar having a glass of wine with the postman, he had heard Berthe's voice in the kitchen.

"One moment please, Madame Maubi."

The "please" had made him prick up his ears and, keeping his gaze fixed absently on the postman, he had listened.

"I should like to have a look in your bag."

"But, Madame . . ."

She must have suited the action to her words, since Madame Maubi protested:

"You have no right to do this. I forbid you . . ."

Berthe was stronger than she seemed and she had got the better of the cleaning woman.

"I shall complain to the mayor. You think you can do as you please just because you are the boss here. . . ."

"Indeed? . . . And what about this? . . . Will you complain to the mayor of that too?"

The postman, who had not been listening, gave Émile a conspiratorial wink.

"A tin of tunny, a tin of *pâté de foie*, a lump of butter, a tin of peaches in syrup. I'm the one who'll be complaining to the police. . . ."

"You'd do that?"

"I'm entitled to, aren't I? I can tell you, I've been watching you for a long time. I wanted to make quite sure. Are you going to try and say you don't get enough to eat in the house?"

"It's not for myself."

Madame Maubi spoke in a dry voice. She didn't ask to be forgiven, didn't apologize.

"It's for my daughter, who's married a good-for-nothing, and my husband refuses to help because she did it without his consent."

"It's not my business to feed her either. You can go. Maubi will continue to work for us, but I don't want to see your face in this house again. Is that clear?"

"Are you going to tell him?"

"Who?"

"My husband."

There was a silence. Berthe must be working out that although she could easily replace the woman, a new gardener would cause her much more trouble.

"I shall tell him I no longer need your services."

"Nothing else?"

"Now go. But first put back what you have stolen."

They were not to see Madame Maubi again, except in the distance, and if Maubi suspected the truth, he gave no sign of it. He too was attached to La Bastide, where he had already been working before Big Louis arrived.

Émile was relieved, for an upheaval in the household might have upset his plans.

Berthe said nothing to him. It was a matter that was no concern of his.

Next day he heard her telephoning to Cannes, to a domestic agency.

". . . It doesn't matter. . . . Resident or nonresident. . . . She doesn't need any special training. . . . It's for the heavy work. . . ."

Berthe appeared to have decided to take on an extra member of the household, which, with the ever-increasing clientele, was beginning to become essential.

They saw, first of all, the arrival of a Polish woman, as strong as a horse, who eyed the kitchen around her as if to size up an enemy. An hour later, she was already on her knees, scrubbing the tiles with a brush.

She had been given the attic room beside Ada's. During the night they could hear her moving about, and Émile knew that Berthe, like himself, was listening. Then the noises stopped. They had heard no footsteps on the stair, no door opening and shutting. Yet next morning the room was empty. In order to ensure that nobody would oppose her departure, the woman had left by the window.

Berthe telephoned again. The agency sent a woman of about thirty, who squinted and appeared to be permanently on the verge of tears.

This was the one they kept, however, for she never stopped working and above all she lowered her eyes in a docile manner whenever Berthe spoke to her.

Little was changed, after all, apart from the fact that the new woman, whose name was Bertha, but they now called her Marie, managed to get up before Ada, without an alarm, and was nearly always the first downstairs. Madame Lavaud made no changes in her habits, contenting herself with an occasional shrug at the uncomely face of the woman imposed upon her as companion.

Easter was approaching. There were two residents and others had booked rooms by post.

It was better for the house to be kept busy, from now on, for it made the time of waiting seem less long. Ada above all was becoming nervous, and if the others noticed nothing, in Émile's eyes she was taking on the appearance of a cat expecting kittens. Sometimes she wandered around in circles, had occasional black-outs.

"What are you thinking about, Ada?"

"Nothing, Madame."

To cheer her up he would make the signal to her, after lunch. She had a special way of creeping to his side with curious humility. Each time, one might have thought she was silently asking his permission and, when she was in her place, one almost expected to hear her purring with contentment.

Sometimes, increasingly often, a shiver would run through her as she lay motionless, her eyes open. Hoping to encourage her, he would say:

"Only two months to go."

Then, only six weeks, one month.

If Émile had been asked how he proposed to organize his life with her when it was all over, he would have had difficulty in replying. To tell the truth, he did not think about it.

Certainly Ada was part of his plans, since she had been at the origin of what was about to take place. He did not envisage parting with her, and probably she still had the same importance.

At least so he supposed. In reality she existed, and that was all there was to it. She formed part of his life, both of his present life and of his future life, but he did not know in what capacity.

It was rather as if Ada had been superseded. The game was no longer being played on quite the same ground. Or again, at a certain moment, on account of Berthe. Ada had acquired an importance which was not really her own.

Émile sometimes reflected that he would no longer need to go and take his siesta in the Cabin, that Ada would sleep with him in the big walnut bed, that they would go upstairs together, in the afternoon, without hiding from anyone.

It was not, however, these images which he called to the rescue in moments of vacillation. It was in the past that he would delve to find his reasons, and even, more often than not, in the past in which Ada had not yet appeared on the scene.

It was no longer a question of causes, motives, still less of excuses. It was a matter of life and death to be settled between Berthe and himself, and it was urgent for one of them to win.

Who knows what Berthe might not be engineering all on her own? She had not accepted the situation with a light heart. A cold rage must be gripping her from morning to night, and nobody grows used to living with rages of that kind.

She said nothing, made no complaint. She had not even complained to her mother. Out of pride.

And, out of pride as well, she was bound to want it to change, at any cost.

He was suspicious, was careful not to eat just anything that came to hand, which was easier for him than for her. He was in the stronger position. It was he who reigned in the kitchen, and he had had plenty of time to bring his plan to maturity.

Easter was too soon, for there would not be enough disorder around them. Disorder was one of his trump cards. One does not react in the same way on a quiet Sunday as when there are forty guests on the terrace, people drinking at the bar and filling every corner of the house.

He must get through the period of calm, following the holidays, without impatience, must wait for the first flood of tourists.

He sometimes felt tired. It was inevitable. But he was conscious of having achieved what few other human beings have the courage to achieve: ten months, soon eleven months of preparation under the mistrustful eye of Berthe, sleeping each night in her bed, without giving himself away on one single occasion.

Wasn't it only natural to regret that there hadn't been any witnesses?

EIGHT

While he was at the wheel of his truck, threading his way among the obstacles and the commotion of the Rue Louis-Blanc, and then, higher up, as he skirted the cemetery wall on his way to Rocheville, yet another wave carried him forward.

He was not posing to himself, not putting on airs. If that had happened to him occasionally during the course of the past few weeks, rather as some people burst into song in the dark, he had rediscovered today, ever since waking up, the same contact with people and things which he had known in his childhood.

On the kitchen doorstep, for example, with his cup of coffee in his hand, he had taken in the scenery, had become one with it, and since then, along the road, at the market, in the harbor, he had not ceased to be an integral part of a fine Sunday.

On his way he looked at the old reddened stones of Mougins on the hill, a new petrol pump beside which a small girl was playing with a doll, peasants in their Sunday best coming down the road as far as the bus stop.

Everything was linked together, living in an ample and serene rhythm. He turned to the left, and along the pebbly road which led off up the hill, pine trees sprang into the air, here and there allowing a glimpse of the Flat Stone which evoked a warm memory for him.

He did not hurry toward his destiny, and it was without haste, without feverishness that he drew up, singing in snatches, in the silver-colored truck, opposite the kitchen door.

He climbed out. Only four yards separated him from the door. There was nobody on the terrace. He did not expect to see anyone on it at this hour, and he had caught sight of the straw hats of the two residents, Mademoiselle Baes and Madame Delcour, floating along hedge-high in the lane to Pégomas.

As usual the two leaves of the olive-green painted shutters were scarcely ajar, so as to let in just enough light, while at the same time forming a barrier against the heat.

He opened one of them. He almost spoke, said a name, any name, the name of the first person he would see, so accustomed was he to there being someone there, male or female, to help him unload the crates.

For once, the kitchen was empty. It struck him all the more forcibly that the only sign of life, a strange vibrating life, was the lid of an enormous saucepan in which water was boiling.

He went into the dining room, where the bar was, which occupied almost the whole of the ground floor. He had been expecting to see Berthe there busy writing out the menus, in her corner by the bay window.

There was nobody there, and on one of the tables lay the pale blue jumper he had seen Mademoiselle Baes knitting.

Disconcerted, he strode over to the foot of the stairs, cocked his head to listen.

He couldn't understand it, anyway didn't stop to think. This, in fact, was the only moment of real panic, which had no connection with what had been planned.

It did not occur to him that this was the hour at which, especially on Sundays, La Bastide appeared at its emptiest. A hotel is like a theater, with its life in the wings on the one hand, and life in the auditorium on the other. On both sides of the curtain a certain time is needed for everything to get into step, and, for instance, when the first spectators come into the half-lit auditorium, an uninitiated person would scarcely be able to believe that a quarter of an hour later all the seats will be filled.

In the wings, too, among the stage hands bustling about, the actors waiting in their dressing rooms, a sort of miracle has to take place each night to ensure that everybody is on stage when the curtain goes up.

At La Bastide, everybody had more or less his fixed task. It was possible that Maubi had gone to fetch some vegetables from the kitchen garden, that Eugène, the new waiter hired the week before, was changing and combing his hair before everyone went to his post.

For each one in particular his absence was explicable, but what gave the house an unreal, disquieting atmosphere was the absence of everybody at the same moment.

For a few seconds he genuinely lost his hold on himself.

"Madame Lavaud! . . . Ada!"

He bounded up the stairs, opened the door of the first bedroom, then the second, which was the two Belgian women's. Finally, in the next room, he came across Ada dusting.

"What's happening? What are you doing?"

She could not understand what he was so excited about.

"There was a telephone call from some people in Marseilles to book two rooms. They are on their way and Madame told me . . ."

"Where is she?"

"Isn't she downstairs?"

"And Marie?"

The one with the squint, who was really called Bertha and whom they had rechristened. Not he. His wife, annoyed at a servant having the same Christian name as herself.

"I thought she was in the kitchen."

He went down, found Marie in her usual place, looking as if she had never moved.

"Where were you?"

"In the toilet."

It was idiotic. He was annoyed with himself.

"And Maubi?"

"He's gone to get some tomatoes."

"Eugène?"

"He must be there. . . ."

She didn't say where. There was nobody besides himself who had noticed the momentary void and been affected by it.

"Help me unload the truck."

He was busy carrying the crates when Berthe and Eugène came out of the Cabin, and for a brief moment his sense of unreality returned. Because the Cabin served as his meeting place with Ada, an association of ideas had just taken place in his mind.

His wife ignored him. Standing in front of the building, she was giving orders to which Eugène was listening attentively.

It was simple. Everything was simple and he had been wrong to allow himself to be thrown off his balance. In fact there had been not one, but two telephone calls from people to say they were coming. Berthe made no mention of them to him, merely announcing later, as she sat down at her table to copy out the menus:

"Seven extra."

Apart from the couple from Marseilles, a family with three children was on its way from Limoges, and must at that moment have been somewhere on the road between Toulon and Saint-Raphaël.

Berthe had gone to make sure the Cabin was in order for the new guests, bringing sheets and towels, and taking not only Madame Lavaud but Eugène as well to help her make the beds.

Émile finally came back to reality again, annoyed at having been afraid without any reason, regretting it all the more because Berthe appeared to have noticed. There were a thousand nuances in her way of looking at him. At times, as with Émile's mother, it resembled the studied attention of someone with weak eyes trying to read small print. At others, it carried a trace of suspicion.

On some mornings she affected an air of melancholy and dignity, and one might have thought she was ready to trample on her pride so as to forgive him and take up their former life.

Her most common expression was one of loneliness bravely borne, the attitude of a woman who is doing her duty toward, and in spite of, everyone, and bears without complaint the burden of the entire household.

There was resignation, too, and more seldom a touch of indulgence, which irritated Émile even more. On these occasions she seemed to be calling the world to witness:

"My husband is young. Men remain children for a long time.

He is infatuated with this girl and it will take time for it to pass. He is not responsible. One day, he will come back, and then he will find me again."

Today it was another note again, which he knew too, one tinged with irony:

"My poor Émile! You think you are a man, without realizing that you're just a schoolboy, that I can read your thoughts behind your stubborn brow, that I know all. . . ."

Madame Know-All! Usually it made him beside himself with rage. This morning, he had been too disconcerted by the emptiness of the house.

Thank God she would not be looking at him much longer with one of those expressions of hers, and he was going to prove that, however superior she might feel to others, she had been mistaken all along the line.

He went up to change, and on the stairs he met poor Ada, who must have been wondering how he was going to do it. Émile's decision having been made, in fact, on the Sunday of the episode of the *cassoulet*, when Berthe had been so ill, it wasn't so difficult for Ada, whose eyes met his at that moment, to guess the method he had chosen.

She knew the date which had been fixed. He had begun by counting in months.

"In three months . . ."

"In two months . . ."

Then in weeks.

"In three . . . in two weeks . . ."

And he had ended by murmuring soothingly:

"On Sunday!"

He hadn't mentioned the time to her, nor the risotto. Wasn't she something of a witch? At heart, she sometimes frightened him. She seldom spoke a complete sentence and often, when she came to him during the siesta hour, she did not utter a word.

She expressed herself principally with her eyes. People who didn't know her took her at first for a deaf-mute, and when he had seen her in the early days in the pine wood this had been his first impression as well.

She belonged to a different world, the world of trees and animals, and he suspected her of knowing things which the common run of mortals do not know. He would not have been surprised to learn that she could foretell the future, or that she knew how to cast a spell.

Who knows if she hadn't cast a spell on Berthe, if it were not because of her that, unknown to himself, Émile was acting in the way he was?

Fortunately he had become drawn, little by little, into the mechanism, into the routine of summer Sundays. From his kitchen, where he cleaned the calamaries with his own hands, so as not to lose any of their ink, he could hear the first cars drawing up. It wouldn't be long now before somebody called out gaily:

"Is Émile there?"

The customers enjoyed calling the landlord by his first name, putting their heads around the kitchen door, and, in the case of the more intimate ones, coming in and handling the fish.

"Well, Émile, what's good today?"

It was worse for the ones who came with friends who didn't yet know the place. The latter used to try to show they felt at home.

"Come and have a glass of *rosé* with us, Émile. Come on!"

He would wipe his hands on a cloth, slip around behind the bar. It was all part of the job.

He had to make three trips that morning, gaining a brief respite from the heat of the oven.

Six customers, out of the ordinary run, arrived early, young people from Grasse on their way to Cannes for a football match, who had decided to have something to eat on the road. They had been misdirected and, dressed in their Sunday clothes, they were trying to affect an air of self-assurance, aware at the same time that they had come to the wrong hotel.

Seeing the menu and the prices, they had almost gone away. Then they had held a whispered council and had ended by ordering some *bouillabaisse* and *vin rosé*.

They were on their third bottle and were talking and laughing loudly, determined to have their money's worth.

The two Belgian women were at their usual table, while the family from Limoges, after a look around the Cabin, had installed themselves on the terrace. Émile had slipped a little packet into his pocket, which he had only to open at the right moment.

He knew the motions he had to go through. It was now a purely mechanical affair. The moment for reflection was past, let alone the moment for hesitation.

The empty packet would burn in a second in the flames of the range, and there would be no trace left.

There would be three of them permanently in the kitchen, for a good hour more: Madame Lavaud, Marie, and himself. Ada and Eugène were waiting on the tables. Maubi was dealing with the wine, sometimes outside, sometimes in the cellar.

Once or twice, before finally sitting down, Berthe would come in to glance around, without saying a word. The best thing was not to look in her direction.

In any case, it was too late.

"Three *bouillabaisses*. Three!"

Maubi had just passed through the kitchen to go down to the cellar, and it was then, as Émile was serving the portions into the dishes, that a thought struck him, so simple, so obvious, that he wondered how it had not occurred to him during the previous eleven months.

Madame Harnaud!

He had foreseen everything, except her. In his mind's eye he had placed her in Luçon with her sister and her niece, as though she were destined to remain there eternally.

Now this was wrong. He knew her well enough. Berthe had not been alone in buying Émile. The mother had taken part in the transaction and perhaps, even, she was the one who first had the idea.

Already, when he was in Vichy and it had been suggested that he should go . . . Big Louis had written the letter, certainly, but hadn't his wife prompted it?

She knew her husband was ill. They were going to be alone, two women, in this Bastide with the fittings not yet finished and the clientele nonexistent. . . .

Émile remembered Madame Harnaud's discreet way of going upstairs, each evening, after the death of Big Louis, so as to leave him alone with her daughter.

What hope was there that this woman, once her daughter was dead, would stay on in Luçon without coming to defend what remained partly her property?

She would come running, no doubt about it. For the moment, she trusted Berthe to keep an eye on Émile. With Berthe gone, she would be forced to take on the task herself.

All this imprinted itself in his mind in the space of a few seconds. His forehead was bathed in sweat, because of the heat from the range, but it seemed unhealthy to him now, like the sweat when one has a fever.

With Berthe, there existed a kind of pact, and he no longer needed to hide from her to make Ada come to the Cabin.

His mother-in-law, on the other hand, was not in the pact and he had deluded himself in imagining that he could simply bring Ada down one floor and put her in his bed.

He had already found the solution. It didn't frighten him. If he had accepted it once, there was no reason why he should not accept it a second time.

It simply postponed the moment of his liberation. He would have to wait years, two or three perhaps, at all events many long months.

He knew by heart the sentence he had read in Dr. Chouard's consulting room, and the words came back to his memory:

"The difficulty of making a precise diagnosis explains the frequency of successive acts of poisoning by the same individual, who can trust that he will not be brought to account until the day when the recurrence and similarity of the episodes provide a clue for the diagnosis."

He must not worry about it at this moment. The other business would be dealt with in its own good time. At all events, since he possessed the solution, he would take both time and all the necessary precautions.

Ada was coming in and going out, bringing in empty plates, carrying others away. From time to time, through the door of the kitchen, the shutters of which had been opened wider since the sun had moved around, he went to glance out onto the terrace to see what point the customers had reached.

He saw Berthe sitting in her place, the new waiter, Eugène, going over to her, being waylaid before he got there by a customer asking for a little more of the sauce of the *bouillabaisse.* Thus it was Ada who had to take his wife's order.

It was of no importance. Eugène would have done it just as well, since it was only a question of carrying a dish.

Before Ada came back, he took advantage of the fact that Marie was looking the other way and Madame Lavaud was in the scullery to pour the powder onto the plate of *risotto* and to burn the paper. It was done as quickly, as smoothly as a conjuring trick.

He was almost certain that Berthe had not ordered any hors d'oeuvre. She seldom had it on Sundays, both so as to save time, for she had to be finished before the customers in order to make up their bills, and because she liked lots of the calamaries.

They did not take her a dish, but, to simplify matters, just her helping on a heated plate.

"Risotto?" he asked Ada, who seemed all of a sudden to have turned a more lifeless color.

She nodded.

"For Madame?"

He had avoided saying "my wife" ever since the word had lost its meaning.

What was passing through his head at that precise moment was not exactly what could be called a thought. It did not reflect a decision, nor even a desire. It was more like the snatches of a foreign language one picks up at random when one turns the tuning knob of the radio, coming from a distant station which one cannot find again afterwards.

Why shouldn't there be images in the air, too, ideas, or scraps of ideas which come from God knows where and which we pick up for the space of a second without knowing what they refer to?

While Ada was turning around, plate in hand, to go back to the terrace, he had just seen her as she would be at thirty-five or forty years old, perhaps fifty, a sort of dark-skinned witch who would frighten children away.

"*. . . the frequency of successive acts of poisoning . . .*"

123

He had said nothing, had thought of nothing. Scarcely an image, springing from nowhere for an instant, which he had straight away dismissed. He had other matters on his mind. He was not living in the future, but in the present.

It was no longer merely the day or the hour. It was the minute. He arranged a dish of *bouillabaisse* fish for three, added, as an afterthought, a little hogfish, handed the dish to Eugène, who was waiting.

He wondered whether it had been a mistake, a few minutes earlier, to go onto the terrace to see what Berthe was doing. Had she noticed it?

He mopped his brow, not with the cloth, but with his white apron. Ada would be back with another order. A minute. A few seconds.

She did not come back. It was Eugène who had had time to return.

"Two risottos."

"Who for?"

"The Belgian women."

He served them, and immediately afterwards felt an urge to light a cigarette. His hand was barely trembling, but it was trembling. The servant with the squint was coming and going as if nothing were happening. Madame Lavaud was sitting in the shade, with some peas in her lap.

He had to go and see. Maubi passed behind his back, with a load of bottles. As soon as he had seen, Émile would pour himself out a drink, as his throat was dry.

He had only four steps to take, he counted them, then raised his head. Berthe's table was the last on the left, by the bay window of the dining room where there was nobody else, for in summer all the customers preferred the terrace.

He had his cap on his head, his cloth in his hand.

Suddenly, despite the sun, the colors, the movement, the commotion, the gesticulations of different people among themselves, the laughs and the raised voices, it was Berthe's eyes on his that he found.

The gaze was fixed on him, calm and hard, devoid for once of irony, and one might have thought his wife knew Émile was about to appear, and at what precise point, that she had prepared that look in advance to receive him.

He did not know what had happened, nor what was happening, but he was already sure that it was Berthe who had won. Doubt became impossible when, opposite her, at the same table, with her back to the kitchen, he recognized the head of Ada, her shoulders, Ada who was at this moment eating the poisoned risotto.

"Two lamb cutlets! Two!"

He preferred to see only her back, not to be obliged to look at her face. He imagined Berthe's voice.

"*Sit down.*"

Ada, standing, not knowing what to do, not daring to protest. The plate pushed toward her across the table.

"Eat!"

She was eating. The plate was already almost empty. Émile went back into the kitchen to put the cutlets on the grill. The flames, which had burned the paper packet a little while before, made the meat sizzle, and brought pearls of blood to its surface.

". . . *the symptoms develop an hour or two after ingestion of the poison . . .*"

". . . *painful vomiting, at first alimentary, then consisting of bile and blood, is followed by colic; abundant serous diarrhea, in rice-water particles; violent thirst; constriction of . . .*"

At all events, it was too late. Berthe had just told him so, without having to move her lips, with nothing but a look.

He was not allowed to intervene. That would have meant . . .

"Three meringues glacées! Three!"

He took the ice from the refrigerator, remained for a moment with his face exposed to the cold air.

"Two coffees!" said a voice behind him, which riveted him to the spot.

It was Ada. She was waiting for the two coffees. She was looking at him as the big yellowish dog must have looked at its master.

Did she expect something from him? He could do nothing for her. She belonged to the past.

He avoided her eyes, went on with his work, filled the dishes and put them on their trays.

He heard Eugène's voice in the dining room.

"The bill for number 12."

That meant that Berthe had taken her place beside the window and had begun totting up the figures.

". . . *the symptoms develop an hour or two after ingestion of the poison . . .*"

It was better not to be there. Even if he took his siesta in the Cabin, there would be somebody to call him. He was not sure of being able to keep his head. Already he was no longer capable of looking Ada in the eye, as she came and went silently, her face devoid of expression.

He sought for a plausible reason to leave as soon as all the customers had been served. He could find none. He lacked lucidity.

Then, there was Berthe standing in the doorway. There were three witnesses: Madame Lavaud, Marie, and Maubi, who was pouring himself out a drink.

"You haven't forgotten the football match?" Berthe was saying, in a natural voice.

He stammered:

"Just a moment . . ."

Madame Lavaud and Marie were capable of pouring out the coffees and putting the meringues on the plates.

Berthe was right. It was high time to leave for Cannes and to mingle with the crowd attending the football match.

She would see to everything. It was better that way. When he came back, it would all be over.

There wouldn't be so very much changed, either, since they had never stopped sleeping in the same bedroom.

He went up there to put on a white shirt, a pair of light trousers, and to run a wet comb through his hair.

He left by the back way, to avoid Ada, started the truck up with such haste that he was already halfway down the hill before he noticed that he had not released the hand brake.

Noland
3 July 1958